# MURDER
## AT THE
# MONUMENT

A SMILEY AND McBLYTHE MYSTERY

Published by Jubilee Publishing, LLC
Ebook ISBN: 978-1-958252-37-6
Paperback ISBN: 978-1-958252-38-3

Cover design: Streetlight Graphics
Editor: Teresa Lynn, Tranquility Press

# MURDER
## AT THE
# MONUMENT

A SMILEY AND MCBLYTHE MYSTERY

# BRUCE
# HAMMACK

## Books by Bruce Hammack

### The Smiley and McBlythe Mystery Series

Exercise Is Murder, prequel
Jingle Bells, Rifle Shells
Pistols And Poinsettias
Five Card Murder
Murder In The Dunes
The Name Game Murder
Murder Down The Line
Vision Of Murder
Mistletoe, Malice And Murder
A Beach To Die For
Dig Deep For Murder
A Killer On Christmas Cay
Hemlock And Homicide
Murder At The Monument

### Other Mystery Series

### Detective Steve Smiley Short Mystery

### The Fen Maguire Mystery Series

### Star of Justice Series

See my latest catalog of books at brucehammack.com/books.

# Chapter One

Steve directed his first words of the day to his coal-black giant schnauzer. "Did you hear that, Le Roi? The cops found a body in the reflecting pool where the battle of San Jacinto took place. If I remember my Texas history, that battle took place in April 1836."

The announcer had already moved on to a story of snarled traffic on several of Houston's freeways. A click of a button on the remote was all it took to still the chatter coming from the small television in the kitchenette.

Steve put on his sunglasses, picked up his half-empty mug of coffee, and moved to the door of his lock-off apartment. Le Roi brushed his left pant leg, showing his willingness to protect and serve.

"Let's see if Heather and Princess are up yet." Le Roi didn't respond, but Steve knew the dog liked the idea of socializing with the German shepherd.

The odor of sage and other spices hit him as soon as the door swung on its hinges. "Good news. They're up and cooking breakfast."

Heather spoke as they came within earshot. "Do you mind taking Princess outside with Le Roi?"

"Only if you'll warm up my coffee." He felt the bar surface to make sure it was uncluttered before setting his mug on it for Heather to fill. "What are you and Princess doing today?"

"I have meetings until eleven, then I'll call the contractor to check on the progress on our new homes. After that, Princess, Rasheed, and I will have lunch and go to the lake."

"You're going to see Bella and Adam?"

Heather gave an affirmative answer and asked, "Do you two want to come along?"

He couldn't think of a decent reason to refuse the invitation. "Getting out of the house is a good idea. What's the weather going to be this afternoon?"

"The same as it's been every day for the past week—sunny, hot, and humid."

"Perfect. The dogs can have a swim in the lake."

His porcelain mug met the marble countertop, making a near-silent clunk. This told him his full mug was in front of him. A waft of Heather's two-hundred dollar an ounce perfume mingled with the aroma of coffee. She asked, "Why don't you bring your bathing suit? We could all go swimming in the lake. I'm sure Bella would swim with us. Sometimes I think she's part dolphin."

"Not a bad idea," said Steve. He turned to go but stopped. "Did you hear the news report about the body they found at the San Jacinto Monument? They pulled it out of the reflecting pool."

"No. I haven't had the news on this morning." She paused. "Why did you mention it?"

Steve answered the question as he shrugged. "No reason, other than it's an interesting place to kill someone. Have you ever been there or seen photos of the monument?"

"I'm from Boston and have been all over the world. I've seen enough monuments to last me a lifetime."

"You'd like this one. It's the tallest obelisk in the world. Looks like the Washington Monument, complete with the long pool of water at the Lincoln Memorial."

"It can't be taller than the monument in DC."

"Fifteen feet taller," said Steve. "Since you're still on a half-day work schedule, we should go there."

Heather took an extra few seconds before she asked, "Are you bored?"

Steve's inclination was to tell her no because he loathed sounding sorry for himself. It wasn't his fault he lost his career as a homicide detective, his wife, and his sight to a senseless crime, but those were the cards life dealt him, and it was up to him to play them as best he could.

After reconsidering the question, he gave a straightforward answer. "I hate to admit it, but I think I am bored, and so is Le Roi. We both like to work and—"

Heather cut him off. "You're already dressed. Come with me to the office today. You haven't been there since we all returned from Argentina. That was six months ago."

Steve lifted his mug of coffee. "Come on, Le Roi and Princess, let's pretend to chase a bad guy in the backyard and then we can pretend we're going to work."

Heather gave her dog the command to go, and Princess strutted off with Le Roi to the French doors leading onto the back patio and the yard beyond.

Steve opened the door but gave them the command to wait. Their muscles quivered with anticipation until he released them with another command for them to search. Toenails scratched on the flagstone patio as both dogs ran for the far corners of the fence. They each sprinted to patrol their section with noses to the ground. Le Roi was at full gallop when he slammed on the brakes and let out a series of deep barks. Princess abandoned her area and joined him, responding with barks of her own. Both stood erect, twitching with desire as Steve commanded them to back away from the fence.

Heather joined Steve on the patio. "What scent did you use today?"

"Bucky Franklin's."

"No wonder they look like they could tear the fence down."

Heather's response wouldn't make sense to most people, but Bucky was public enemy number one in Steve's book: a dirty ex-cop, arsonist, and swindler looking at a long prison sentence if he and Heather could ever catch him. Steve took some consolation in knowing they'd made Bucky's life miserable by making sure arrest warrants for him remained active.

Steve rewarded the dogs for their good work with treats and an extended game of tug of war with a short length of thick rope.

Le Roi weighed a hundred pounds while Princess came in at a svelte sixty-five pounds. That added up to a lot of biting and dragging power between the two trained police dogs, companions, and bodyguards.

Le Roi, The King, always played the gentleman and didn't overpower Princess by pulling her across the yard but held his ground while she did all she could to jerk the rope from his jaws.

Following the short but intense workout, Heather called them in for breakfast. The rope fell to the ground when Steve gave the command. They joined him, one on each side, and moved with him when he started toward the back door.

The singsong, heavily accented voice of Rasheed, Heather's driver, greeted them as they came through the back door. "Good morning. Heather tells me we have a day of work and play ahead of us."

"More play than work for me," said Steve, with an unintended touch of longing in his voice.

The former professor of philosophy countered with, "It is said that changes will find you, whether you seek them or not."

Steve tilted his head and asked, "Did you make that up?"

"It is also said that a fertile imagination can fool many fools. You, Steve, are no fool. My muse speaks to me, and I write things down."

Heather spoke from the kitchen. "Rasheed, have you eaten?"

"Thank you for asking, but I find the selections at Jose's Food Truck are temptations I cannot resist. I'm still making up for many missed meals in my native land. While in prison there, I had no choice but bread and water. Now that the menu is unrestricted, I prefer Jose's breakfast tacos."

Heather directed her words to Steve. "Your plate is on the bar. I've given up trying to keep you from sneaking bites of sausage to Le Roi and Princess. I cooked two extra small links, one for each of them. Please don't give them anything else from the table."

"You forgot something," said Steve.

"What's that?"

"You didn't cook a link for Max."

Max, Heather's persnickety Maine coon cat, rubbed against his ankles as Heather said, "He's on a diet. No sausage for him until he loses some tonnage."

Steve held up three fingers in the Boy Scout salute. "I promise on my honor as an Eagle Scout, I'll not give him anything off my plate."

Heather released a huff. "That would mean more if you hadn't dropped out of scouting when you turned fifteen."

"That wasn't my fault. They didn't like my suggestion that

Boy Scouts and Girl Scouts should combine. It would have made camping much more interesting."

Heather's only response was to offer him jelly.

Steve finished his breakfast, went to his room, and spoke to Le Roi. "Bring me your vest and I'll get you dressed for the day." The words sent the dog scurrying to the bedroom. Steve attached all the straps, stood, and took the harness in his left hand. After retrieving his white cane and instructing Le Roi to carry a small gym bag in his teeth, the two made for the garage.

Multiple doors of the Mercedes SUV opened and closed, then seat belts clicked. Steve sat in the back seat and wondered what he'd do until 11 a.m. while Heather worked. Perhaps he'd call Leo, his former partner at Houston Homicide, and see what he knows about the body found at the monument.

# Chapter Two

Heather's thoughts turned to business as Rasheed guided the SUV to the hub of her growing empire, a four-story building with her name on it in The Woodlands, Texas. She stopped the thought in mid-think. Empire was too strong of a word. Her father had a true business empire. She searched for other words to describe her company. Well-diversified, honest, profitable, and growing came to mind.

Her most recent project, a yet-to-be-completed upscale lakeside housing, business, and recreational development, was the biggest risk she'd ever taken, and it was on the verge of producing more revenue than predicted. It had taken every ounce of knowledge, training, energy, and luck to pull it off, but the success also came with a high price tag. The road back from physical, mental, and emotional exhaustion proved almost as difficult as what caused her breakdown.

A big revelation came when she realized she didn't have to micromanage the senior staff she had so carefully hired and trained. In her absence, they'd carried on and worked with amazing competence, sometimes improving on her ideas and procedures.

Perhaps the biggest breakthrough came when she no longer looked at life as competing with her father. She'd emerged from a mental meltdown and now found herself bonded to her father in ways she didn't think possible. He still lived in Boston but cleared his schedule to spend thirty minutes talking with her at the beginning of her business day. One of the things that pleased her most about those conversations was that they weren't always about business.

She turned to Rasheed. "What's on your schedule today?"

"I'm meeting with another job applicant to discuss the philosophy and expectations of your company."

"What department?"

"Legal."

"What's this person's area of expertise?"

"Artificial intelligence."

"Your initial impression?"

Rasheed smiled. "She has gams that would make burlap stockings look good."

Steve erupted in laughter from the back seat.

Rasheed glanced to his right with a grin parting his lips. "Forgive me. I read a gritty detective novel last night, and that's how the private detective described the legs of a woman who walked into his office. He used many other descriptors, but that one stuck in my mind."

"It's in mine, too, now," said Steve, still chuckling.

Rasheed took his turn again. "To give you a less flippant answer, I have met this woman who seeks employment only once, and it was a brief encounter."

Heather played along. "If you think she can make burlap stockings look good, I want to meet her."

They arrived and rode the elevator up to the fourth floor.

As always, the sight of two stunning dogs wearing special vests caused heads to turn. Those familiar with Le Roi and Princess dropped what they were doing and admired the animals. Heather had nicknamed the regal walk of the two of them together The Royal Promenade.

The staff in Heather's outer office all but swooned when Le Roi and Princess entered. She knew there would be a heated discussion on whose turn it was to take them for a mid-morning walk.

Rasheed went to his office while Steve passed out pleasantries.

Heather went into the oversized office she shared with Steve when they were working a case and settled into the chair behind her desk.

Steve settled himself at his desk and took out his laptop computer. He opened it, but didn't put on headphones. She asked, "What are you going to do this morning?"

"Scroll the news for something interesting. If I can't find anything, I'll try to write another chapter in my book."

"How long have you been writing this one?"

"Six months."

"How many chapters have you written?"

"One, plus three paragraphs."

"Ah."

"Yeah. Not much progress, is it?"

"Have you lost interest in writing?"

Steve took a full breath and let it out in a rush. "I need someone to give me a swift kick in the pants. I know the words are in me, but there's a block between my brain and my mouth. I have to dictate it, and I sound like a nervous teenager."

"Who says you have to dictate it? Type it out."

"There's a block between my brain and fingers, too."

Heather folded her hands together on top of her desk. "Have you tried talking to someone about other options?"

"Like who, and what?"

Heather wanted to help but was at a loss. She chose the first person who came to mind. "Call Kate Bridges."

Steve followed a long pause with a frosty response. "Her last name isn't Bridges anymore."

The ringing of Heather's phone gave her an excuse to escape from the touchy subject. She put the phone to her ear. "Hello, Father."

Steve put his headphones on and went into his dark world. Le Roi rose from his oversized dog bed and placed his head where Steve could pat him. Not only was he trained to protect and attack, but Le Roi had also received additional certification as a therapy dog, as had Princess.

Heather listened as her father posed questions about her plans for the day.

"I told you yesterday about the meetings I have planned. Any suggestions about the recommendation from my acquisitions department about purchasing stock in the new AI company we talked about?"

"Make sure your risk assessment people do their homework. There's a rumor going around that another company is going to beat them to the punch with a superior product."

"Text me the name of the company. If the rumor you heard is true, my acquisitions people will have some explaining to do."

"I have a better idea. We both have acquisitions departments with multiple employees. Let's have the heads of each department call each other and trade information regularly."

Heather didn't have to mull over the suggestion. "I love it. As things stand now, you and I are duplicating work."

"Exactly. We're also missing out on opportunities. I don't know about you, but my portfolio is lite in commodities."

Heather broke in. "My group found a copper mine that's being mismanaged. I'm long and slightly overexposed in mining, so I'm not interested."

Her father cleared his throat. "That's the type of synergism I'd like our companies to have. Also, it will save you and me time, and that's the most precious commodity we have."

"I learned that the hard way," said Heather, with a tinge of regret.

The tone of her father's voice changed to something more upbeat. "And speaking of time, are you seeing Jack regularly?"

An unbidden smile came to her face at the thought of Jack, her boyfriend. "He's a wonderful role model for me to follow. He works hard, plays hard, and drops everything when Briann needs him to attend some sort of school function. On the weekends, he sleeps late unless he's hunting, fishing, or we go someplace. And best of all, he's content with the results of his career. Did I tell you he hired another attorney?"

"No. Good for him."

"Jack allows them to work as much overtime as they want but encourages them to enjoy life."

"Is your engagement still on hold?"

"He's not pushing it because of Briann. We want to make sure she's fully anchored with him before I put the engagement ring back on. She still misses her mother and I'm not ready to compete with a memory."

"How is Steve?"

The answer caught in her throat. "He's... here in the office with me today."

"Is there a case for you two to work?" whispered her father.

"Not yet." She turned and faced the window to reduce the chances Steve could hear her.

"I'm concerned. He and Le Roi came to the office with me this morning."

"What's he doing?"

"Scrolling the internet."

"That must mean he's bored. You need to give him and Le Roi something to do."

Heather challenged him. "That's easier said than done. What do you recommend?"

"Is he writing stories about his past exploits in homicide?"

"I think he'd like to, but between Bucky Franklin tricking him into giving away the copyrights, and losing Kate as his writing coach, he's stuck."

Several seconds of silence passed before her father said, "Perhaps he needs a change of scenery. Is there a spare office you could put him in?"

"There's several on the third floor, and even more on the second. I bought this building with the intention of my company growing."

"Here's an idea that Steve might go for," said her father. "Ask if he'd like to have an office to come to whenever he wants to write."

Heather shifted her gaze from side to side as she considered the proposal. "That might work. Steve never worked from home before he lost his sight. I think he's one of those people who believes home is for living and someplace else is for work. I'll feel him out on the idea of coming here to an office. If he doesn't turn me down, I'll have a place set up for him tomorrow. He can come and go as he pleases."

Heather checked the time. "Thank you for the talk, Dad. I know you have a busy day ahead of you. I'll call tomorrow and let you know how my conversation with Steve went."

Heather checked her phone; she still had time for a brief talk with Steve before her first meeting. She looked his way as he pulled noise-canceling headphones away from his ears.

"How's your dad?" asked Steve.

"He's well, except for being worried about you."

"Me? The only reason he'd be worried about me is if you told him something that made him worry."

It was typical of Steve to know she was up to something. He lifted his chin and asked, "What did you tell him?"

"That you were bored and needed to take up knitting or crochet."

Steve chuckled. "Why not watch repair and give me a real challenge?"

Heather shot back with, "Why not get back to writing?"

"To paraphrase an old song, I've lost that loving feeling, except it's not loving someone, but my urge to write I've lost. I sit down with good intentions, but can't find the motivation. I tried other writing coaches and nothing works."

Heather moved to his desk and sat in a chair in front of it. "Perhaps if you treated it more like a job, you'd have better luck."

"Is this some sort of reverse psychology trick you're trying to pull?"

"It was Dad's idea. He suggested you might get back in the groove of writing if you had your own office, someplace other than your home."

Steve grumbled. "If you hadn't noticed, I'm sitting at a desk, in an office, that's not in my home."

"Not this office. You need to try writing in an office that's all yours. If we're not working a case, you think you're inter-rupting me."

"That's because I am. This is where you come to run your company."

Frustration peppered her next words. "Listen closely and don't interrupt. When we're working on a case, this is our office. You have your desk, and I have mine. When we're not working on a case, you need a separate office, a place you come to write your stories."

"That would be a waste of money." He tilted his head. "Are you trying to get rid of me?"

Heather flicked away the comment with her hand, even though he couldn't see her. "I'm going to explain this to you one more time. You have two jobs. When we work cases, we share this office. If you want to write, you can use an office on the third floor. Several are open, and I don't plan on using them for years."

"Why didn't you tell me you had unused offices to begin with?"

She shook her head in dismay. "If you don't like the third floor, there are even more open offices on the second."

Steve rubbed his chin. "It seems you and your father have my life planned out. What time do Le Roi and I report to work?"

"If you want to ride with me and Rasheed, we arrive here at seven-thirty in the morning."

Steve reached for his earphones. "Your personal assistant is about to knock on the door. When do you want an answer?"

"Now."

"Then we need to discuss a suitable salary and benefits package for me and Le Roi."

Heather felt the corners of her mouth pull up. "Your salary is all the money you make selling the books you write. Your benefits include free transportation to work and treats for your dog."

"Let's see," said Steve. "I'm currently earning nothing. You should be able to double that."

"It's a deal," said Heather. "You'll have suitable office furniture and coffee as a bonus. I'll even order a new bed for Le Roi, so you won't have to lug his current bed up to our office when we have a case."

Steve held out a hand for her to shake and said, "You drive a hard bargain, Ms. McBlythe."

"As do you, Mr. Smiley."

The door opened, and it was time for Heather to shift gears. Steve leaned forward. "I'm still calling Leo this morning to get the story of the body they found at the monument."

"Do you want to use your new office?"

"That would be nice."

# Chapter Three

With his workplace secured, Steve rose to leave as her head of acquisitions arrived for an appointment. Heather made a phone call while he made small talk with her employee.

"You're all set," said Heather. "Rasheed is pestering one of the ladies in the outer office. He'll take you to your new office."

Rasheed was exchanging pleasantries with a receptionist but broke away from the conversation when Heather's door opened. By his tone, Steve wasn't sure if Rasheed was being friendly or if he had designs on taking the first steps to starting a harem.

"There you are, my friend," said Rasheed in his heavy accent. "The *other duties as assigned* clause in my employment contract means I'm at your disposal until my interview with the applicant for the legal department takes place."

"When is that?"

"Not until nine-fifteen."

"That's more than enough time," said Steve. "You don't have to stay with me unless I don't have a chair and a desk."

"We shall find the answer to that question together. All I know is the room number. Too bad it isn't 221B."

Steve let out a soft chuckle. "Sir Arthur Conan Doyle would roll over in his grave if I tarnished that number by pretending to be a real author."

Rasheed gave the perfect comeback. "Write better stories and someday Room 307 will be even more famous."

"Easier said than done," mumbled Steve.

The elevator descended, eased to a stop, and the two men and a dog stepped into the hallway. Rasheed said, "All the doors are closed. The word isn't out yet that you and Le Roi are taking an office."

"That's a good deduction. Which way to my office?"

"Go straight, and then we'll enter the outer office on the left. If I'm not mistaken, your office is directly under Heather's."

A door let out a squeak and Le Roi led Steve forward. A woman squealed with delight. "Le Roi! I heard you were coming to join us. I can't believe it." She then said, "Hello, Mr. Smiley. I'm Doris Gray. You probably don't remember me, but I met you when some of the staff came to decorate Ms. McBlythe's home for Christmas."

"I remember your voice, but didn't catch your name. I hope you don't mind me taking an office." He paused. "Is this where I'm supposed to be?"

"This is your new home. We call ourselves the outcasts."

"We? Who's we?"

Rasheed explained. "Doris works for Human Resources, but there's no room for her in that department."

Doris interrupted. "The business is growing, and this suite of offices is where new employees come until there's an office or cubicle for them in their department. Rasheed and I work together to onboard new employees."

Rasheed took his turn again. "There's a conference room that we use for group presentations and also doubles as a break room. Most new employees start off in a private or semi-private office. Doris is the glue that holds everything together."

Steve faced Rasheed. "Where is your office?"

"Next to yours."

Steve pursed his lips. "If I didn't know better, I'd say Heather wants you to spy on me."

"Never, and the use of the word spy brings back many sour memories. I had many spies reporting about me in my home country. The very mention of the word causes my skin to slide along the ground."

Doris corrected him. "The phrase is, *makes my skin crawl*."

Steve groaned. "No one can butcher an idiomatic expression like Rasheed." He shifted his grip on the harness. "Le Roi, are you ready to see our new office?"

"Follow me," said Rasheed.

Doris lifted her voice. "Let me know when Le Roi needs to go outside. I have a growing list of volunteers."

A soft click was all Steve heard to indicate Rasheed had opened the door. He took one step inside and stopped. "What are the room's dimensions?"

"Approximately fifteen feet wide by twelve feet deep."

"How much furniture?"

"A two-pedestal wood desk, an executive's desk chair, two filing cabinets, and two chairs in front of the desk. There's an office phone. Your extension is the same as your room number."

"This is perfect," said Steve, as he nodded with satisfaction. "I'm glad Heather gave me something plain."

"How else can I be of service?" asked Rasheed.

"Give Le Roi and me a few minutes to snoop, then show me where I'm to plug in my laptop. He'll help me remember after today."

Rasheed waited in silence, while Steve used his cane and his dog to familiarize himself with the office. He could tell Rasheed had moved to stand in the doorway by the sound of his breathing.

Accented words came from the other side of the room. "There's a power port built into the top of the desk."

Steve tried out the chair and ran his hand over the top of his desk. "There it is. I'll have no trouble finding it."

"What else do you need?" asked Rasheed.

"Le Roi needs his bed, and I smelled coffee when we came from the hallway."

"Yes, my friend. Your nose did not deceive you. The break room's door is closed at the moment, but I can go to the next floor and get you a cup of Sam."

"It's a cup of Joe," said Steve, as he held up a hand. "And there's no need to go downstairs to score coffee. If the door is closed, I'm to wait. Right?"

"Correct. There's an illuminated OCCUPIED sign that goes on when the door shuts. I realize that won't help you but—

"I'll train Le Roi to recognize it and what it means."

After a few seconds of silence, Rasheed asked, "Is there any other way I can help you before I go next door to my office?"

"I'll bang on the wall if I need you."

"Tapping out messages in morse code is how another professor and I communicated when we were imprisoned back in my native land."

"My morse code is a little rusty, so I'll probably call or send you a text."

A voice sounded from the open door. "Delivery for Mr. Le Roi. One enormous bed for an extra-large dog."

Steve pointed to the floor beside his desk. "Put it here, and thanks."

"Anything else, Mr. Smiley?"

19

"That's all for now. Are you a custodian?"

"Yep. They call me Sonny. I'm the official mess cleaner-upper and broken things fixer-upper. All you have to do is tell Miss Doris or Mr. Rasheed what you need done, and I'll come running."

Steve grinned. "Does that make you a runner-upper?"

Sonny let out a booming laugh loud enough to have inter-rupted Heather's meeting on the floor above. Sonny left the room with his laugh going before him.

Rasheed asked one last time if there was anything else he needed before leaving Steve and Le Roi to settle in. For man's best friend, this took the form of walking three laps in a tight circle in his oversized dog bed and plopping down for a morning nap.

Steve located his computer bag on his desk, right where Le Roi left it. The dog's extreme height meant it took little effort for him to place it where Steve would find it.

The desire to get to work hit Steve hard. It was decision time. Should he call Leo and see what he knew about the body at the monument or get started on a new short story? After checking the time, he opted to give Leo another hour or two before bothering him.

The next decision Steve needed to make was how he would write the story. He had two options: He could type on his keyboard or dictate. Dictation required him to speak words, sentences, paragraphs, and chapter prompts. He also gave prompts for punctuation and special spellings. The software would read it back to him. He even had his choice of voices and accents.

He checked the time and settled in to dictate a short story based on a case he'd worked as a rookie detective. An hour and a half later, it surprised him how much progress he'd made. Le Roi shifted on his bed, yawned, and stretched.

"Do you need to go outside?" asked Steve in French, which was the dog's preferred language.

A soft whimper was the dog's positive response. Steve stood and walked to the opposite side of the desk, where he reached for the handle attached to Le Roi's vest and grasped it with his left hand. The two left the office and took the short walk to Doris's desk.

The gregarious woman asked, "Is it time for a walk outside?"

"His Majesty needs a fire hydrant," said Steve.

"The king's wish is my command." She placed a call, and in a few seconds, a woman's excited voice gushed out an explosion of words, mostly declaring how lucky she was to be seen with Le Roi.

Steve issued a word of instruction. "He won't react to anything unless people are fighting or he smells a scent that he recognizes. If he suddenly sits down, that's his way of telling you he's detected something illegal, like narcotics. If that happens, reward him with praise and vigorous petting. Then, lead him away."

"How cool! He's like a real police dog."

"Only better," said Steve.

Steve returned to his office, closed the door, and pulled out his phone. He told it to call Leo Vega.

It took five rings before Leo answered. "Hello, Steve. How's the man of leisure?"

Steve huffed, injecting a note of wounded dignity to his voice. "I'll have you know, I'm in my new office, slaving away."

"What new office? Did you move from your recliner to the bedroom?"

He responded with, "Unlike someone I know, I don't keep my feet on my desk all morning, waiting for work to find me."

Leo sounded skeptical. "Uh-huh. What's the catch? There

must be a reason you called me. I'm guessing you're bored and fishing for a lead on a nice, juicy murder."

Leo had taken Steve's place as a senior detective at Houston Homicide and knew him better than anyone except Heather.

"For starters," said Steve, "I called to tell you I now have a luxurious office in Heather's building. I'm using it to further my career as an author."

Leo burst out laughing. "Did she clean out a broom closet for you?"

"It's an actual office on the third floor. Room 307. If you don't believe me, come on any workday unless Heather and I are solving a murder for you."

"You're not joking?"

"Nope. I was going nuts sitting in that one-bedroom lock-off. I tried writing here this morning, and the words flowed for the first time since Kate stopped being my coach."

"Do you ever hear from her?"

"Not since she married. That chapter of my life is closed, locked, and I've thrown away the key."

"This may be a strange transition, but how's the dog?"

"Great. Unlike some people I've worked with, he obeys."

"Hilarious. Does he give you leads to murder cases?"

"Not yet. I'm still training him to do that." He sucked in a quick breath. "And speaking of leads on murders, what do you know about the body they found at the San Jacinto Monument?"

"That's not my patch."

"Don't you think I know that?"

"Wow. You must be bored to chase a news headline. It's still a suspicious death that's out of my jurisdiction. The monument is at the very edge of the City of La Porte, which is in

Harris County, but the monument and battlefield are inside a state park, inside a city that's not in my jurisdiction."

"That means state park police have primary jurisdiction. All I'm asking is, do you know any details of the death?"

"Only rumors based on what was on television this morning."

"What are the rumors?"

"That park police found the body of an unidentified man in the reflecting pool on the west side of the monument before dawn this morning."

Steve took in the information. "Was there any mention of the cause of death?"

"The standard line reporters give about no cause of death announced."

Steve's mind whirled with possibilities. "Heather and I may take a trip to the monument tomorrow."

Leo lowered his voice. "I know what that means. You want to discover if this is a murder or not before anyone else does. If by some chance it is, try not to include me. I have more than enough to do without you adding to my caseload."

Raised voices came from the hallway. Doris opened Steve's door without knocking. "Le Roi ran away, Rasheed is interviewing, and I don't know what to do."

Steve came out of his seat. "Call Heather. Tell her to take the elevator and pick me up on her way down. Le Roi doesn't run away unless he's going to attack someone."

# Chapter Four

Heather and Princess stood away from the door of the elevator and allowed Steve, Doris, and an intern named Mandi to enter. Mandi's whole body shook like a stop sign in a tornado.

Heather rested her hand on Mandi's shoulder. "You're not in trouble. Take a breath and hold it in until I tell you to let it out."

Mandi complied. The one thing Heather didn't want was for the young woman to hyperventilate and not be able to recount what happened to Le Roi. When the elevator stopped on the bottom floor, Heather said, "Slowly, release the breath. Very good. Now take another shallow breath and hold it as we walk slowly from the elevator to the exit."

Once outside, the four stopped and Heather asked, "How do you feel?"

Mandi gave her head a dip and returned Heather's gaze. "Much better."

"Excellent. Take your time and tell us what happened."

Mandy gave a weak head bob. "I was gripping the handle of

the thingy attached to Le Roi's vest. We started for the designated puppy potty area when Le Roi suddenly stopped, lifted his nose and went nuts with barks so loud that he scared me half to death." She lowered her head. "I dropped the handle, and he took off like a rocket. I've never seen a dog run so fast or bark so loud."

"Where did he go?" asked Steve.

"To a car on the far side of the parking lot, close to the exit that leads to the street. The car started moving before Le Roi caught it. It was a small SUV of some sort."

Heather asked, "Could you see the person driving?"

"The windows were too dark to see anything but an outline. It could have been a man or a woman."

Steve spoke next. "Take us to where Le Roi broke away from you." He then said, "Heather, get a good grip on Princess's leash. She may bolt."

Heather gave the command for Princess to search. The German shepherd's ears stood up and her nose went to the ground. She pulled hard as they walked an angled path across the parking lot.

"Not much further," said Mandi.

The words had no more left her mouth when the dog surged forward, erupting in a frenzy of barks. If Heather hadn't slipped her hand through the loop at her end of the thick, leather leash, Princess would have repeated Le Roi's escape.

The foursome plus Princess came to a spot on the lot and Heather gave the command for the dog to heel.

"Why have we stopped?" asked Steve.

Heather bent down and examined an object on the ground. "It's a windshield wiper with bite marks on it."

"Bucky Franklin," said Steve. "He's back."

Heather puffed out her cheeks. "Le Roi and Princess both caught his scent. What do we do now?"

"We follow the trail," said Steve.

Heather looked up to see her SUV backing out of her reserved parking space. Tires squealed and smoke billowed from the tires as she realized Rasheed was coming their way in a big hurry.

Steve addressed the group. "There's no need for all five of us to go. Doris, you and Mandi stay here. We'll be back when we find Le Roi."

Heather looked down at her three-inch heels. A woman's voice came from over her shoulder. She turned to see a brown-skinned woman wearing a business suit and running shoes. The woman spoke in a calm, matter-of-fact tone. "I'm a marathon runner and you can't run in heels. Give me the leash and get in the car with Rasheed."

"Do as she says," said Steve.

Heather released her right hand from a two-fisted grip and placed the loop around the woman's outstretched hand. "Who are you?" asked Heather.

"Rasheed will tell you." The woman said as she ran in the direction Princess was pulling her.

Steve hollered, "Get in the car!"

Heather wasted no more time. Her door closed at the same moment Rasheed took off after the stranger and her dog. Both dog and woman ran at a blistering pace while Rasheed activated the car's flashing emergency lights and followed close, but not too close.

Heather kept her gaze on Princess, but directed her question to Rasheed. "Who's the woman?"

"Junani Hasan. She seeks employment with your company."

Heather watched as the woman settled into a seemingly effortless stride. "She's making an excellent first impression."

"You snatched the words from my lips," said Rasheed. "She impressed me greatly, also."

Steve spoke from the back seat. "Check behind you, Rasheed. Don't allow anyone to pass if you can help it. Block the lanes if you have to."

Heather added, "Princess may change lanes or turn without notice."

Block after block, they traveled a serpentine route through an upscale residential area of The Woodlands. Rasheed announced the miles as they clicked by. After six miles, they turned onto a four-lane road.

Heather spoke. "The speed limit here is fifty-five."

"Good," said Steve. "Le Roi is fast, but he can't run fifty-five miles an hour and he's tracking a car that isn't leaving much of a scent on the pavement. I hope he has sense enough to get out of the road."

Approximately two minutes later, Heather saw Princess explode forward and pull with all her might. Junani tumbled onto the asphalt and the loop came loose from her hand. Rasheed had to brake and swerve to avoid the woman, which left Heather's SUV parked sideways in the road.

Rasheed put the car in park and opened his door at the same time. He ran to Junani, lifted the thin woman from the pavement, and carried her to the side of the road.

By this time, Heather had joined them. "Are you all right?"

Junani ignored the inquiry but had something to say through gasping breaths. "Put me down, Rasheed. I'm not hurt. We must follow Princess."

Instead of releasing his grip, Rasheed carried Junani to the car.

"Put her in the front seat," said Heather opening the door for him.

Rasheed deposited her on the leather seat, then gave her a

tennis shoes-to-hair visual inspection. "You've torn your pants and your knee is bleeding."

She narrowed her gaze. "It's nothing. We must find the dogs. Stop staring at me and do your job."

The words broke whatever spell Rasheed was under. He ran to the driver's side and jerked open the door. Heather was still closing her door when he put the car in gear. By stomping on the accelerator and cutting the wheels, he caused the back end of the car to come around.

"I can barely see Princess," announced Junani.

Steve located an unopened bottle of water in the back seat and handed it to Heather. "Give this to Junani."

Heather leaned forward and said, "Take this."

Junani's mind and eyes focused straight ahead. "There!" she shouted.

Heather's gaze shifted to a spot about an eighth of a mile ahead. She squinted. "It's Princess and Le Roi."

Steve asked, "Is Le Roi standing?"

The car rushed forward until Rasheed made a hard, but controlled, stop on the grass beyond the right shoulder. Four doors opened at the same time. Heather rushed to secure Princess, who sat panting at Le Roi's side.

Junani spoke from behind her. "Le Roi and Princess are both panting. They look unharmed but regal. What magnificent creatures."

Steve snapped his fingers, and Le Roi walked toward him and stood by his left leg. "Good boy," said Steve.

A county patrol car pulled up behind Heather's SUV with its emergency lights activated. The deputy sheriff hitched up his gun belt as he swaggered toward the unusual roadside gathering. "Who's the driver of this vehicle?"

Heather responded. "What's the trouble, officer?"

"Do you own this vehicle?"

"My company does."

"I'll need to see your driver's license and insurance card."

"My vehicles are self-insured."

A confused look crossed the officer's face as he took in and exhaled a full breath. "Look lady, just give me your license. We'll discuss the ticket for no insurance later."

Junani stepped forward. "Officer, did you witness Ms. McBlythe commit a traffic violation?"

"Stay out of this and stand back."

Heather smiled at Junani. "Please tell Steve to call the sheriff."

Steve overheard her and grinned. "Do you want me to ask him how many fish he caught last Tuesday?"

Heather turned back to the officer without responding. "Where were we?"

"Almost to the place where you go into handcuffs for refusing to provide a valid ID."

"I never said I was refusing, but I'd like to know why you're demanding it. As my attorney asked, what traffic violations do you suspect me of committing?"

"From the reports I received from dispatch, you broke enough traffic laws in the last fifteen minutes to give me writer's cramps for the next two hours."

"That would be unfortunate," said Heather. "I've had flareups like that in the past. Perhaps we can discuss this misunderstanding, and you won't endanger your wrist."

He held out his hand with the palm up. "What will it be? License or handcuffs?"

Heather heard Steve's muffled laugh but focused on the officer. "I must repeat the question posed by my attorney, and I quote, 'What traffic violations do you suspect me of committing?'"

"Wait," said Junani. "Officer, you're precariously close to

making a serious mistake. She wasn't driving." Junani closed the distance. "You made a rookie mistake of assuming she was driving because she was the first to speak."

Heather released a guffaw followed by, "I was a cop for ten years. We pulled the same joke on rookie officers. I hope there are no hard feelings."

The officer rolled his eyes.

Steve offered his phone to the officer. "The sheriff was busy, but your captain wants to talk to you."

The conversation didn't last long, and the deputy's swagger had evaporated by the time it was over.

Heather took Steve's phone and handed it to him.

"You have my apologies, Ms. McBlythe. I'll be sure to remember yours and Mr. Smiley's names."

Steve extended his hand for the deputy to shake. "You were doing your job, but you need to brush up on the statutes related to self-insured motorists."

Heather added, "It wouldn't hurt if you did role play with seasoned officers on how to handle unusual traffic stops and what to say when people refuse to identify."

Steve said, "If you want help, I'll be on the third floor of the McBlythe building in The Woodlands, Room 307. Call before you come. I'll be writing a story about a murder."

"Really?"

"He's not joking," said Heather. "Twenty years as a cop, most of them as the top homicide detective in Houston, bought him a ton of knowledge and experience."

"Are you two working a case now?"

Steve answered, "That's why my dog ran almost seven miles after a car. We believe the driver to be a man wanted for theft, arson, and attempted murder. Heather and I were, and still are, his target. He's a former cop from Houston by the name of Bucky Franklin."

Heather added, "You can do us a favor by keeping an eye out for a late model, dark SUV with a missing rear window wiper." She pointed. "Le Roi ripped it off the car. Call for backup if you see the car. The driver doesn't play nice."

Steve said, "You'll receive a BOLO on the car and driver as soon as your captain contacts dispatch."

The officer looked down the road. "Was this the last known location?"

Heather nodded.

The officer turned and ran to his car.

Steve sidled up next to Heather. "He'll never catch Bucky."

"No, but I like his enthusiasm."

Steve announced, "If anyone's hungry, Heather's buying lunch."

"Gladly," said Heather. She looked at Junani. "That includes you if you're up to it."

"I appreciate the offer, more than you know, but I must honor my current employer and return to work."

"Of course."

Rasheed made sure Le Roi and Princess were safely in their 'jail cell' in the back of the car and each had a bowl of water. Heather sat in the back seat with Steve. On the way back to the office, she leaned forward and said, "Junani, do you always wear running shoes with a tailored business suit?"

A tinkle of a laugh came forth. "No, but it was most fortuitous today. I broke a heel by getting it stuck in the narrow opening between the elevator and the third floor. My vanity suffered a terrible blow as I had to return to my car and retrieve my running shoes."

"Most fortuitous, indeed," said Rasheed. "Do not quickly dismiss unlikely events. They often point to the path we should follow."

Steve pulled out his phone, called Leo, and told him about

Bucky's reappearance. He also called the sheriff, who already knew of Bucky returning to the area.

Steve turned to face Heather. "Do you need to work in the office this afternoon to make up for this morning?"

"I could, and should, but I won't. I'd rather spend the afternoon swimming."

"Good answer," said Steve. "What about tomorrow? Can you get away by noon?"

"Eleven o'clock. That's my new schedule. Where are we going?"

"To check out an old battlefield and a recent death."

Heather wiggled her eyebrows, even though he couldn't see her. "What a refreshing way to spend a summer afternoon."

Junani leaned to her left and whispered to Rasheed. "Are they serious?"

"Oh, yes. They never pull your arm when they discuss homicides."

"Don't you mean pull the leg?"

Heather and Steve spoke in unison. "He got you."

Rasheed was quick to apologize. "I'm so sorry. It's a game we play to take a common expression and change a word in it."

"Ah," said Junani. "If I'm invited back for a subsequent interview, I'll need to keep on my little piggies."

Rasheed tilted his head. "Little piggies?"

Laughter exploded from the back seat. Heather spoke once she stilled the last laugh. "You've more than earned a second interview. Rasheed will call you tonight."

# Chapter Five

After returning Junani to her car, Rasheed suggested they stop at an enclave of food trucks for an al fresco lunch. Steve's choice was two kosher hot dogs with an unusual assortment of toppings. He ate both, and his shirt came through with no major smears or spots. The same didn't go for Rasheed, whose shirt bore the stains of marinara sauce. A flimsy paper plate overloaded with lasagna caused the culinary disaster. Heather played it safe by ordering a bowl of salad and a heavily buttered slice of garlic bread.

They continued their journey to her massive housing development, which she and Steve would soon call home. If it wasn't for Bucky's penchant for arson, they'd have moved in by last Christmas. It worked out for the best as she added a fourth bedroom, workout room, sauna, and two additional bathrooms to her original plans. She managed to convince Steve to add a third bedroom to his two-bedroom, two-and-a-half bath dwelling. He'd already planned for a home office and would keep his exercise equipment in the garage since he had no other use for the space.

Heather looked forward to seeing the workers' progress and hoped their estimate of two more weeks before completion wasn't tempting fate. She turned her head and shifted in the passenger's seat. "Steve?"

"Yeah. I'm awake."

"Are you satisfied with the security coverage we have on the construction site?"

"I was until Bucky showed up today. We have twenty-four-hour coverage of the backyards with guards and dogs. Motion activated lights flood all sides of the homes. Bella and Adam live next door and he's a light sleeper. Normally, I'd say that was enough. What do you think about getting one more armed guard and dog to patrol inside the subdivision? They could roam the entire peninsula all night."

"I like it. I'll tell the agency to make sure the guards have night vision equipment in case Bucky cuts the power. We're too close to completion to take any chances."

Heather shifted her gaze to Rasheed. "What do you think?"

"Huh? What do I think about what?"

Steve spoke from the back seat. "About Junani. What's your opinion of her?"

"She would be a welcome addition to Heather's staff. She's well educated, has an excellent work history, is multilingual, confident, aggressive when she needs to be, has a delightful sense of humor, and—"

Steve cut him off. "That describes most attorneys who make it past the first round of interviews. What makes her special?"

Heather didn't know where Steve was going with this line of questions, but sensed he was setting Rasheed up for a teasing he'd not soon forget.

Rasheed stammered. "I... uh... she... well..."

"Let's cut to the chase," said Steve. "Do you believe she's a good-looking dame with legs that begged to be looked at?"

Heather slapped her hand over her mouth to cover a laugh.

Rasheed took his time answering. "I appreciate you remembering my newfound fondness of old movies with the reference to dames. I also must remember that your powers of observation are so developed that you sometimes harvest my thoughts." He paused. "My answer to your question is affirmative, and I thank you for planting the image of her long legs in my mind. I look forward to many pleasant dreams."

Steve reached around Rasheed's headrest and patted him on the shoulder. "Good answer, my friend. Not all dreams come true, but if they do, you'll be four aces."

With thoughts of romance in the air, Heather took out her phone and placed a call to Jack.

He answered with a greeting that told her he was alone. "Hello, beautiful. Are you off work?"

"You'll be proud of me. Steve, Rasheed, and I left work early today. We've already had lunch and we're on our way to the lake to see Bella and Adam. There's a swim in our future if you care to join us."

A groan of disappointment sounded through the phone. "I love the idea, but your timing is off. I'm slated to take three depositions this afternoon."

"What about tomorrow afternoon?"

"I shouldn't, but what did you have in mind?"

"A trip to the San Jacinto Monument."

"Business or pleasure?"

"Business, with a dash of pleasure. Steve wants to check out the scene of a possible homicide."

"He must be bored."

"Not as much as he was yesterday. He now has his own office on the third floor of my building. It's his writing office."

Heather paused and took a breath. "There's one more thing I need to tell you that happened this morning. Le Roi caught Bucky's scent this morning. An intern took him outside to potty and he broke free. Princess trailed him for almost seven miles with us following in my car. Le Roi tore the wiper off the back of a car, but Bucky eventually got away."

Jack said nothing for several seconds. "You did all that before noon?"

"Let's see. I also spoke with my father. He told me to tell you hello. I'll probably hire the attorney who ran with Princess when they chased Le Roi." She thought for a second or two. "Rasheed has the hots for the attorney. She runs marathons, and he's partial to long legs." She hesitated. "Oh yeah, I'm going to hire another security guard with a dog to stay behind the fence and gate that blocks our peninsula from intruders."

After a moment's pause, Jack said, "If it was anyone else, I wouldn't believe that story. I'm taking off tomorrow to go with you."

"Be at the office by nine? I'd love to buy you lunch. Steve ays he knows of some good seafood place close to where we're ,oing."

"Count me in. I may have to work Saturday to make up for t, but you're having way too much fun for me to miss out."

"Perfect."

Jack's next words came over the sound of his office phone ɔeeping. "I'll work late tonight but call you when I get home. Are you packing?"

"That word has two meanings. If you're asking if I've started boxing things to move, then the answer is not yet. If you're asking, do I have a pistol in my purse, then that's a defi-nite yes. I don't go anywhere outside without Princess on my left and a pistol within easy reach."

"Good. Keep it that way."

The call ended with the usual salutations. Heather looked to her left as Rasheed drove with both hands on the wheel at the ten and two o'clock positions. She thought about the woman seeking employment and how she could show her gratitude.

"Rasheed," said Heather, then paused.

"Yes?"

"Junani ruined her pants and shoes this morning. I want you to find a way to replace those items and deliver them to her with my letter of appreciation and a check to compensate her for injuries."

He glanced her way with trepidation in his eyes. "My weakest area of knowledge is women's clothes. Surely there's someone more qualified than me to complete this task."

Steve spoke up. "To be a successful detective, you need to think creatively. If you don't want the assignment, I'll do it."

"No!" He lowered his panicked voice. "What I meant to say was, I will complete the task."

"It will be good practice for you," said Heather. "You have three days to complete this, or Steve and I will do it."

Steve added, "Consider delivering the clothes to her gift wrapped. Over supper would be a gracious gesture."

Heather watched as Rasheed swallowed hard. "I find my mouth and brain are suddenly dry."

The rest of the trip passed in silence as they all seemed to withdraw into their own thoughts. That changed when Rasheed turned the car from the new four-lane county road that ran past her development.

Steve noted the turn. "I can tell by the road noise, we're close to the entrance. Did you get the repair done to the stonework?"

Heather looked ahead. "It looks good as new. May the Lord save us from drunk drivers operating delivery trucks."

It took several more minutes for Rasheed to complete the

journey. A strip of land jutted into Lake Conroe. An ornate metal gate and fence separated the peninsula from the rest of the development. Rasheed punched in a code, and the gate swung open. He drove through onto a paperclip-shaped concrete street. Two completed homes, technically duplexes because they shared a common garage wall, stood off to the right. The first showed no signs of life and belonged to Bella's parents, who hadn't yet moved from Puerto Rico. The second belonged to Bella and her husband, Adam.

Rasheed turned onto the second driveway, brought the SUV to a stop, and announced, "I'll get Le Roi and Princess out and take them for a quick walk in the future pocket park."

"It's going to be a baseball and soccer field," said Steve.

Heather groaned. "Here we go again." It was a long-running discussion between Steve and her over what would be the best use of the land in the center of the hairpin shaped section of land. Heather favored a park with extensive landscaping, while Steve thought a multipurpose sports field could serve adults and children living in the homes on nearby streets. Perhaps a compromise was possible.

All thoughts of parks and softball games disappeared as Bella opened her front door. The young woman was the closest thing Steve had to a daughter and had become a younger sister to Heather.

Despite the cut-off jean shorts, tank top and bare feet, with her long, ultra-blond hair draped over one shoulder in a silvery braid, the statuesque young woman in her early twenties resembled a Nordic goddess. The hug Heather received was like so many she'd received before... longer than necessary, but worth every second. Bella could convey more with a simple hug than Heather had words to describe. Then it was over, but the feeling of the bond between them remained.

"Uncle Steve," said Bella as she went to deliver the next

hug. Steve's embrace usually lasted longer, but Heather wasn't jealous. After all, it was Steve who was mostly responsible for returning Bella to her biological parents after being kidnapped as a child.

"Hello, Heather."

The deep voice came from behind her and belonged to Adam, Bella's husband.

She spun to embrace him and was struck again by the Ken-and-Barbie looks the two possessed, especially when they stood side-by-side. Adam also had abandoned shoes on this June day that felt just shy of sweltering. A Hawaiian shirt and Bermuda shorts completed his ensemble.

It was a quick embrace. Adam, the shy, bookish counterpoint to Bella's extroversion, gladly let her be the hugger in their family. Bella claimed Adam could talk a blue streak when they were alone but preferred to stay in the background when the number of participants exceeded two.

He broke tradition by speaking. "Your homes look wonderful."

She responded with a smile. "My contractor said two more weeks, but we know how schedules go."

"I'm learning all about schedules."

The response seemed odd, but Heather dismissed it.

Adam cast his gaze to Bella as she unwrapped her arms from around Steve. "How's the master detective?"

"A little bored," said Heather, "but I've taken steps to get him back around people. He now has an office in my building. He was having a hard time focusing on his stories from home. After so many years of going to work, it's natural for him to equate leaving home and going somewhere else as a trigger to work."

"I'm surprised you have any offices left, the way your company is growing."

"I overbought and leased out much of the building. As my needs have increased, I worked with my tenants to find them other places. Sometimes I bought or built them something that better fit their needs."

"There may come a day when I'll ask you to lease me an office," said Adam.

"Are you considering changing careers?"

"Not careers, but perhaps where I work." He grinned. "Forget I said anything. I work best from home."

Rasheed joined them, instructing the two dogs to sit. Instead of going inside the house, Heather said, "I don't know about the rest of you, but Princess and I are going to look at the latest additions to the neighborhood. Does anyone else want to go?"

The vote was loud, quick, and unanimous. Five humans and two dogs would go next door. Four would look, and one would use all his other senses to snoop.

Steve gave a word of warning to Heather. "Hold on tight to Princess and I'll do the same with Le Roi. I doubt if Bucky's been here, but if he has..."

Heather finished the sentence for him. "Our dogs may pull us into the lake."

Bella asked, "Why would they do that?"

Steve said, "To answer that, it will take a long time, some shade, and tall glasses of iced tea or lemonade. For now, I'd like to tap my way around my new home." He searched the ground in front of him with his cane. "By the way, are you two busy tomorrow? We're going to the San Jacinto Monument."

Bella giggled. Adam cleared his throat. "Uh... We could be at Heather's office by nine."

"Perfect," said Heather. "It's just an information-gathering outing. Nothing special except fantastic fresh seafood."

Steve sniffed the air. "I smell glue."

Bella asked, "What does that tell you?"

"In southern climates, they usually use adhesive to glue engineered hardwood flooring to the concrete slab. Flooring is one of the last steps to complete a construction project. It tells me moving day is right around the corner."

# Chapter Six

Bella and Adam walked into Heather's office at 9:10 a.m. They held hands, which wasn't unusual, but Bella's cloudy eyes and the down-turned corners of her mouth told a tale that all was not right.

Adam did the talking, instead of his bubbly fashion model wife. "Good morning, Heather. Your personal assistant told us to come in. I hope we're not interrupting anything."

"Not at all. I finished all I'm doing today. We'll swing by Steve's office and pick him up on the way out. There's six of us going, so we'll need to take two cars. I brought both of mine. Rasheed will drive one, and Jack can drive the other."

"If you don't mind," said Adam. "Bella and I will take our car and follow you."

Adam's suggestion confirmed Heather's suspicion that something had caused Bella's silence. She wanted to know what it was, but discretion told her to wait. She'd allow the couple to reveal the problem when they were ready.

Heather kept her tone light. "That's fine. I'll put Steve up front with Rasheed while Jack and I hold hands in the back seat."

Bella found her voice. "Thanks for understanding."

Adam's shoulders dropped a fraction of an inch, and the tempo of his words increased. "We parked close to you. Come down when you're ready. We have all day. If we get separated, keep going. We'll catch up."

The couple made a quick exit as Heather gathered her laptop and a profit-and-loss report she might or might not read before tomorrow and hooked the leash on Princess's collar. She then said farewell to the staff in her outer office and made for the elevator, where she traveled down one floor.

Steve waited for her in his new office with the door open. "Right on time, but you're alone. I thought Bella and Adam were going to your office first."

"They did. Something's going on with them." She related what she observed and heard.

"Ah," said Steve. "I think I know what it is." He didn't sound worried, which puzzled her even more.

"She was so bubbly yesterday," said Heather. "It's like all the fizz in her went flat overnight."

"All they need is some time alone and a change of scenery."

Rasheed came out of the office next to Steve's. "What a pleasant change of pace to go to a battlefield and a monument. I studied the battle last night, and it's most remarkable. Are Bella and Adam running late?"

Heather fielded the question. "They're taking their car and going by themselves."

A simple nod of Rasheed's head acknowledged he'd heard the slight change of plan and accepted it with no further explanation.

No one said anything else, except a quick goodbye to Doris

as they passed her desk. Once in the elevator, Steve announced, "I called Leo. He'll meet us at the reflecting pool."

Heather considered his words but made no response, her thoughts spinning like a merry-go-round. Leo meeting them meant he had information to share concerning the recent murder. Did they have a case to solve? What changes would she need to make to her work schedule? Would the case cause one more delay in moving into their new homes?

She took a deep breath and stilled her thoughts the way the therapist taught her.

The ding of the elevator as it reached the ground floor signaled the clearing of her mind, then another thought surged in. Leo was meeting Steve for a reason only a few people knew about or would believe. Steve possessed a rare gift that helped him solve murders. Associative chromesthesia was the technical name for this little-known ability. When Steve went to the site of a suspicious death and someone spoke the name of the victim, he perceived the color red if it was a homicide scene. In the case of death by natural causes, or if the victim was still alive, Steve remained in his dark, colorless world.

Heather looped her arm in Steve's and slowed his pace as they approached her SUV. Rasheed had walked ahead and waited for Le Roi and Princess at the rear of the car. Both owners released their dogs at the same moment, and they ran to Rasheed, bounding into the back of the vehicle.

Heather whispered as Rasheed took off Princess's leash and Le Roi's vest with the attached handle. "Whose idea was it for Leo to meet us?"

Steve whispered, "Mostly Leo's. The preliminary cause of death is drowning, but they haven't ruled if it was an unfortunate accident, suicide, or homicide. They found the body in the reflecting pool on the west side of the obelisk. The water in the lungs matches that in the pool, but the victim had a head injury and a high amount of alcohol and some drugs in his system."

"Do you want to be alone with Leo when he says the victim's name?"

"You're my partner. What's the problem with you hearing it?"

"It freaks me out every time you see red after I say the person's name."

"Me, too. I didn't ask for this so-called gift."

Jack arrived and completed the guest list for the outing. After a quick kiss, Heather and her former fiancée settled into the back seat. She asked, "Was Briann upset I didn't invite her to come with us today?"

Jack's response began with a laugh. "Fat chance of that. I'm officially off her radar screen for everything but hunting, fishing, and teaching her how to run a law office. Otherwise, it's school and her friends."

"What about boys? Any developments on that front?"

"Not yet, and I'm counting on you and Mom to help me navigate those waters." He paused. "It would be so much easier if I didn't have to go through the years that end in t-e-e-n."

Rasheed spoke from the front seat as he accelerated onto I-45 South. "Those can be years of emotional tumult, both good and bad."

"Mostly bad for me," said Steve. "Or at least I thought they were bad. All it took was an untimely zit or a bad haircut and I'd stay in my room and pout."

Jack said, "Thirteen was my worst year. I was late hitting my growth spurt and was chubby. You wouldn't believe the number of bad rhymes and limericks I heard that began with *Fat Jack.*"

Heather put in her contribution. "I took martial arts at age twelve to help me survive boarding school. No one is as vicious as a girl from a family with a title after their name. The daughters of once well-off dukes or duchesses were the worst."

Rasheed took his turn. "It is said that our teen years prepare us for the rigors of life, but I don't believe it. Mine hardened me so I could endure until I discovered inner peace found in logic and reasoning."

Steve nodded. "Well said, my friend." He then added, "It's a shame some people never outgrow their teens."

A pensive mood settled over the occupants of the car and lasted until they passed Houston's Bush Intercontinental Airport. Heather watched as a 747 winged its way southeast, the general direction they needed to travel to get to their destination.

Rasheed skillfully negotiated the interchange between I-45 and Houston's Loop 610. It wasn't long before the highway made a sweeping turn south and the traffic thickened.

Steve's sensitive sense of smell alerted him to their location. "We must be near the Port of Houston. I smell petroleum."

Rasheed confirmed his thoughts. "We approach the bridge over the ship channel. The number of large trucks has increased on the roadway. Many transport gasoline and other petroleum products, and I see enormous storage tanks."

"Get used to seeing them," said Steve. "They stretch from here all the way to Galveston Bay."

Heather added, "Oil made Houston the city that it is."

Since Steve had lived most of his life in the metroplex area, Jack asked him, "How would you describe Houston?"

"It all depends on which part you're talking about," said Steve. "Where we're going is in a suburb of Houston, part of the metroplex. The monument and battlefield are in La Porte. The land is low, flat, and prone to flooding during hurricanes and tropical storms. Expect to see oil refineries and chemical plants from here to Galveston Bay and numerous other bays. It was a strange place for a battle, but it worked out well for the Texians, as they were called."

Rasheed countered with, "Not so for the Mexicans."

Steve confirmed the assessment. "It was a stunning victory followed by wholesale slaughter."

Heather tilted her head. "Was it that bad?"

Rasheed had the answer. "The Texians were avenging their losses at the battles of the Alamo and Goliad, where Santa Anna, the president of Mexico and chief general of the army, spared none of the wounded or captured, even those who surrendered."

Steve's phone rang, which put an end to the history lesson. "Hello, Leo.... Yes... I'll ask Rasheed. How many more miles?"

"Eighteen."

"We should be there in about twenty-five minutes. Where do you want to meet?"

Steve said he knew the spot and ended the call. "Take Independence Parkway and turn on Park Road 1836. Find a place to park near the reflecting pool."

"That's a clever number to give to the road. It's the year the battle took place."

Anticipation grew in Heather as she caught sight of the obelisk long before they arrived. It stood out like a huge, gray spike made of stone, shooting upward on a flat plain. A closer look revealed a huge decorative star capping it.

Rasheed followed the directions of the voice coming from the car's navigation system and eased to a stop alongside Leo's car. Somehow, Adam and Bella had kept up through busy Houston traffic and parked next to them.

A blast of hot, muggy air hit Heather the moment she opened her door. Adam came out of their Lexus SUV looking sporty in shorts and a knit shirt, but with one complaint. "My sunglasses fogged the moment they hit the hot air."

"Mine, too," said Heather.

Steve exited the same side of her car as Heather and teased, "I didn't notice."

"No more blind jokes," said Heather. "You're limited to one a day."

Princess joined Heather with her leash dragging behind her. Le Roi followed and sat by Steve's left leg. Rasheed asked, "Shall I take the dogs to the trees and let them do what comes naturally to them?"

Heather looked down at the German shepherd's pleading eyes. "I'll take Princess. You and Le Roi can find your own tree to hide behind."

Bella released a giggle, which Heather took as a good sign. An even better one came when Bella circled her car and gave Leo a two-armed hug. They were catching up on the antics of Leo's six children as Heather and Princess walked to a clump of trees.

Jack went with them and asked, "What's the plan for the day?"

Heather allowed Princess to go to the end of her long, leather leash and pick out a discreet place. "Steve, Leo, and I will stay somewhere near and talk shop. When we're finished, we'll meet you four at the monument where all of us will stay out of the sun, watch a movie in air-conditioned comfort, ride an elevator to the top, and take in the view. When we arrive back on ground level, you'll buy me a cold drink and we'll go to the gift shop, where we'll purchase a souvenir for each other."

"How long before you three and the dogs join us?"

Heather turned and gazed at Steve and his former partner as they walked to the long, narrow body of shallow water. It acted as a mirror to the towering obelisk on this hot, cloudless, mostly calm day. "Steve's looking for a murder to solve. I expect it to take between fifteen and thirty minutes before we join you. There's plenty of displays to look at inside."

Princess finished her business and bounded back with head held high. Heather gave her a word of praise and looked at the monument. "It must be half a mile from where we are."

"And to think," said Jack. "That's how far the Texians ran through tall grass before engaging the Mexicans, and they still took them by surprise."

Heather looked at him. "You've been here before?"

"Just a field trip when I was a kid. I had a few minutes last night and read a little about the battle. I don't think anything the three of you discover about the body in the water will be able to hold a candle to the battle that took place here."

# Chapter Seven

It wasn't long before Le Roi slid his head under Steve's left hand and brushed against his leg. Leo's voice sounded. "I don't know why you waited so long to get a dog."

"I didn't want to settle for anything but the best. Le Roi wasn't born yet."

Leo let out a huff. "Do you realize your dog has made my life miserable? Ever since you brought him to the house, all I've heard from my kids is how much they want a dog like him. It's hard enough feeding eight of us, let alone one more who prefers steak."

"There's plenty of small rescue dogs. They're not as particular as Le Roi."

"We tried that once. The dog needed rescuing from my children and ran away."

Steve wanted to get on with what he came for, and raised his voice so everyone could hear. "Leo won't be able to stay and go to the monument with us."

"Some people have to work for a living," muttered Leo.

Ignoring the comment, Steve continued, "I hope you don't

mind, but Heather and I need to discuss something with Leo. Unless you enjoy looking into the reflecting pool and sweating, I recommend you go to the monument and check out the exhibits in comfort."

Heather spoke up. "Adam, you and Bella should have space in your car for Rasheed and Jack. Do you mind taking them?"

The question received a positive reply, and the group divided.

The tone of Leo's voice changed. "Let's walk down to the spot where they pulled Dan Clay out of the water."

Steve gripped the handle on Le Roi's vest and walked beside Leo with Heather and Princess on Leo's other side. "Tell us about Dan Clay."

Leo spoke in a flat tone, like he was reading from a policy manual. "Thirty-eight-year-old white male. Divorced, but didn't remarry. Mother deceased. Cancer. Father is Stewart Clay, owner of Clay Oil who lives in the River Oaks area of Houston."

Heather said, "That's where Adam used to live, before the family lost their fortune." She shook her head. "Never mind, you already know that story." She corralled her thoughts and said, "I've heard of Stewart Clay but never met him. My father has had dealings with him and described him as an old-school oil man. He's not lacking for money, or enemies. His current wife is Lisa Roberts-Clay."

Leo nodded and continued, "Dan, the victim, has one sister. Cindy Clay. She's an environmental activist who blames the oil industry for her mother's death."

Steve took in the information then had another question. "Did Dan have a romantic interest?"

Leo had the answer. "There's almost always a woman in the mix if you have big money but Dan was playing the field."

They came to a stop and Steve asked, "Is this where they pulled him out?"

"This is it. Water in his lungs, booze and pills in his belly. The water matched the sample they took from here. They found his car in the parking lot across the highway on the ship channel side of de Zavala Cemetery. That's where the Texians spent the night before the day of the battle, under live oak trees on the banks of Buffalo Bayou."

Steve set his feet shoulder length apart. "Say his name."

Leo said the name distinctly. "Dan Clay."

Silence enveloped the location as a shudder coursed through Steve's body and he whispered, "Bright red."

Several long seconds passed in silence before Steve squared his shoulders. "Someone went to a lot of trouble to kill Dan Clay and make it look like an accident or a suicide. Is that how you see it, Leo?"

"So far, it's being ruled as a suspicious death. We three know it's no longer suspicious. Someone murdered Dan within a few yards of where we're standing."

Heather chimed in. "There needs to be a more definitive ruling of homicide, or this case will die on the vine. One or two weeks of intense investigations by overworked detectives seems to be the norm. If there's no substantial progress, interest will wane, and supervisors will reduce the manpower allotted to the case."

Steve added to the process. "Without evidence of some sort popping up, the detectives' supervisors will take out the words 'possible foul play' and replace them with 'probable suicide' or 'accidental death.' The case will go unsolved and the killer will literally get away with murder."

Heather had another thought. "That's what usually happens, but Stewart Clay could bring a lot of pressure to bear on the investigation. Big money has a way of influencing politicians, who in turn put pressure on the police."

Steve faced Heather. "What's important about Dan's car being parked between here and the ship channel?"

"It gives validity to the theory that he killed himself."

"What else?"

"He may have met someone in the parking lot. They walked through the cemetery, crossed the highway, and that person pushed Dan into the reflecting pool. He hit his head and drowned."

"Any other scenarios?"

A few seconds passed before Heather said, "It's possible there were two or more people involved. They got Dan really drunk, came here, and drowned him in the reflecting pool. Someone else could have driven Dan's car and left it in the parking lot. Two vehicles would explain how the killer or killers left the crime scene and Dan's car remained in the parking lot."

"Excellent," said Steve. "You're thinking like a detective again. Let's see if we can do something that might help in the future."

"What did you have in mind?"

"The scent from the time of the murder may be gone, but let's see if Le Roi or Princess can pick up on something."

"It's been days and there's no telling how many people have walked on the ground around the pool."

"I know it's a long shot, and I don't expect it to work, but one, or both of them, may remember a scent if they smell it again. Le Roi had no trouble smelling Bucky across the parking lot."

"Yeah, but you trained him for months to react to that scent. It was the repetition that caused him to attack and chase."

Steve turned to face her. "Do you have a better idea?"

"No."

"Will a twenty-minute walk with your dog do any harm?"

"Yes. I'll be sweaty."

"How about a ten-minute walk? You go left and I'll go right."

Leo put in his contribution. "And I'll go to my car and run the air conditioner on full blast."

Steve turned to face his former partner and friend. "Have you figured out how you're going to get Heather and I involved in this case?"

"I was hoping you'd have one of your brainstorms."

Steve leaned on the top of his cane. "As much as I hate to wait, Heather and I can't barge into this case without a client. If the park police and whoever they get to assist them haven't made an arrest in a week, we'll work out a plan to have one of the family members hire us."

"A week?" said Heather. "That's when we're supposed to move into our new homes. I had it all planned out."

Steve let out a low grumble. "We have the rest of our lives to live in those homes. I talked to your PA. She's lining up the moving company to pack and transport all our possessions as soon as the homes are ready for occupancy."

Steve spoke in a tone of complete seriousness. "You've been worrying too much about our homes and moving. I had to make sure you didn't have a setback. Now, it looks like I may need your brain fresh and ready to focus on this murder."

Heather tented her hands on her hips. "What have you done?"

"You're getting away from everything for a few days to rest."

"How far away and how many days?"

"Five days, if you don't count today. Don't worry about how far. We had fun planning everything."

"We?" asked Heather. "Who else is involved in this plot to save me from myself?"

"Not too many people. There's your father, Jack, Briann, and her latest best friend, Cammy. Oh yeah, Jack's mom is coming, too."

He gulped a breath. "By the way, Rasheed and I will drop you and Jack at Hotel Galvez this afternoon. Your father should be on the ground by now in Conroe. He's picking up Jack's mom, Briann, and Cammy before flying on to the regional airport on Galveston Island. You're going on a five-day cruise starting tomorrow afternoon. That was your dad's idea. He wonders if it's time to sell some of his cruise line stock or buy more. He wants a firsthand look at one of their ships and its operations. One of the company's vice-presidents will be on board for three of the five days. I suggest you and Jack find something else to do on those days."

Leo chuckled. "Heather's standing slack-jawed with her hands on hips. She looks like a grouper about to swallow a bait fish."

Heather held up her hands. "Wait. I'm having sensory overload. Are you telling me you planned out my life for the next week?"

"It's called a vacation. I've been on one since January. Now it's your turn."

The plan left Heather shell-shocked, so Steve kept talking. "You're not off the clock yet. You and Princess have a job to do. She'll sniff while you walk one side of the water and Le Roi and I take the other."

"Wait. What about Princess while I'm gone?"

"What about her? She and Le Roi will go home with me and Rasheed after we drop you off at the hotel. Your PA packed everything you need for a week and your dad is bringing everyone's luggage."

Heather stumbled over her next words. "I was going to do background on Dan Clay's family members."

"Bella, Leo, Rasheed and I will work on that while you're gone. Don't worry, there will be plenty for you to do when you get back."

"I feel like I'm shirking my responsibility as your partner."

"That's false guilt, but if it's going to stress you too much to relax, find out all you can about Stewart Clay from your father. He'll enjoy doing a bit of long-distance snooping with you."

Leo broke in. "You two can stand in the sun flapping your gums, but I need to leave. Call if your dogs solve the case without your help."

Steve extended his hand, and Leo gave it a hearty shake. "Call me if the park police get lucky and solve the case."

"How can they?" interjected Heather. "They don't even know this is a homicide."

# Chapter Eight

Heather, Steve, Le Roi, and Princess climbed the stone steps of the monument and received the reward of cool air as they entered through the door facing northwest. She paid the modest entry fee, and they soon joined the rest of their group. Jack took one look at her and said, "I'd give you a kiss, but you look a little wilted."

She looked up at him. "I'll look more presentable tonight at the hotel."

A wide smile came across Jack's face. "Did you like your surprise? Steve insisted on telling you. He, your father, and my mom arranged the whole thing."

"You'll have to work hard to top this one."

Jack's eyebrows lifted. "It's your turn next to surprise me."

Heather took a step forward and whispered, "That's a challenge I'll gladly accept."

Bella's giggle sounded from behind Heather and broke the spell of the moment.

"It's good to hear you laughing again," said Heather.

"Sorry I was such a fuddy-duddy earlier. I'll tell you about it later. The movie is about to start."

Rasheed led the way and leaned forward in his seat throughout the movie. It depicted the events preceding hostilities, the battle itself, and how it brought about Texas becoming an independent nation, even though that status lasted only a few years.

Her driver summarized the battle as they walked out of the theater. "Unbelievable! The Mexicans lost six-hundred and fifty soldiers to only nine Texians during the 18-minute battle and what followed until nightfall. I still don't understand why Santa Anna didn't have sentries posted in the middle of the afternoon."

Steve offered a weak answer. "Some things are just meant to be."

The entire group loaded into a small elevator and rode to the top of the obelisk. Workers had made small windows on three sides of the observation deck. Rasheed marveled at the craftsmanship completed in 1939. Adam stood beside him and added, "I can't get over how flat the land is and how many ships, refineries, and chemical plants you can see from here."

Bella had a different perspective on being so high. "I'm not crazy about heights, and this place is spooky. My stomach turned a flip when I looked down at the reflecting pool."

Steve leaned on his cane. "I'm ready to go down if you are. Observation towers aren't my favorite attractions anymore."

Jack and Rasheed chose to stay and look a while longer when the rest of their party returned to the first floor. The elevator wasn't particularly fast, so they had time to talk. Bella took the lead as she gripped Adam's hand. "I owe you an explanation about why we weren't decent company this morning."

Steve interrupted. "You had a doctor's appointment this morning."

Bella's eyes widened. "How did you know?"

"Maggie and I had several visits to her OB-GYN like the one you had today. I could tell by the disappointment in your voices what was wrong."

Heather thought of slapping herself on the forehead. How could she be so dense? Instead, she asked, "How long have you been trying?"

"We've not taken precautions, and there wasn't a need to before we married. This was the first time my body and the calendar fooled us. We found out this morning that there's no little blessing yet."

"Is there cause for concern?" asked Steve.

"Not yet," said Adam. "Bella's doctor told us to allow nature to take its course for another year. She recommended we travel to places we've never been before."

"That sounds like a prescription we all could use," said Heather. "Even if it doesn't lead to little blessings with dirty diapers."

Steve held up his hands. "Being blind and messy diapers doesn't sound like a delightful combination."

The elevator slowed to a bumpy stop. Heather asked, "Is anyone else hungry?"

"Starving," said Bella.

"I know just the place," said Steve. "There's a restaurant in Seabrook called Tookie's that has amazing seafood. It's a block off the highway, four blocks from the bay, on the way to Galveston."

Adam looked at Bella. "What would you say if I suggested we go on to Galveston too and stay the night?"

Bella's head bobbed like a cork on a windy day. "We need to follow the doctor's advice. I've never been to Galveston."

Following a quick stopover in the gift shop, where Jack and Rasheed rejoined them, the group returned to their cars and began the next leg of their journey. With the air conditioner blowing cold air, they skirted salty waters on a road that split the city of La Porte like a cleaver. They arrived at Seabrook's TOOKIE'S RESTAURANT and allowed the dogs to sniff a couple of palm trees.

Steve lifted his head and inhaled deeply. "Ah, the smell of Trinity Bay, Galveston Bay, and grilled seafood. This brings back wonderful memories."

The sound of heavy traffic on an overpass dulled conversation until the group scaled the stairs leading to the restaurant built on telephone poles. Once inside and seated, Steve gave a commentary. "Even though it was out of our way, Maggie and I used to come here. This place is close to NASA and it wasn't unusual to hear interesting conversations, especially during happy hour."

Jack said, "Speaking of happy hour, a cold beer sounds good to me. What about you, Heather?"

"I'll take the first drink off yours and have a glass of wine with my meal."

The server took drink orders then scurried to fill them. Jack leaned into her and asked, "Do you and Steve have a case to work?"

"Speak up so everyone can hear," said Steve.

"I asked if you and Heather have a case to work after meeting with Leo."

Rasheed added, "I'm curious about that, too."

Heather gave a guarded answer. "After consulting with Leo, we determined there was a murder, but we don't have a client yet."

Rasheed added, "*Yet* is the key word. It tells me you will get a client. How do you propose to do that?"

Steve leaned forward. "That's a trade secret. I could tell

you, but..." The rest of the common phrase hung in the air unspoken.

After a few seconds of silence, Bella asked, "Will you need help?"

"Will your schedule allow it?" asked Steve.

"I have a photo shoot for next winter's line of clothing and boots, but that's days from now."

"Good," said Steve. "You and Rasheed can help me gather background information on the victim's family. Depending on what we discover, we may add other people to the list of people to investigate."

"This excites me," said Rasheed. "I'm used to doing research, but not to solve a murder. I feel like I'm turning into a real gum-sandal."

An explosion of laughter sounded before Heather took pity on him and said, "It's gumshoe, not gum-sandal."

Rasheed wagged a finger at her instead of telling her he disagreed. "I looked up the etymology of the word and it means shoes with a rubber sole. This allowed a person to walk quietly to avoid discovery. I know it's slang for detective, but everyone wears sandals in the place of my birth. I changed the usage to include people from other countries, where sandals are the preferred footwear."

Steve said, "That's a very rational explanation. You may be ahead of the world by adding new words to the lexicon."

"Do you really think so?"

"No, but I like the way your mind works."

"We all do," said Heather. "What does that agile mind of yours tell you about Junani Hasan? Should I add her to my legal team?"

Rasheed's gaze shifted to a spot on the far wall. "I find I'm unable to give a rational answer. My hands produced excessive moisture, and my tongue stumbled when I interviewed her."

"Perhaps I should interview her," said Heather.

"That would take a load off my chest."

"Do you mean *a load off my mind?*"

"I don't think so. My heart races and my mind shuts down when I'm near her," he admitted sheepishly.

The server returned with drinks, and the conversation shifted to talk of the upcoming cruise. Jack took the lead as Heather settled into a state of excited contentment. She wondered how she could be so lucky to be surrounded by these people at the table and those who would go on the cruise with her. Her gaze rested on Steve as she allowed her thoughts to run wherever they wanted. Her words followed. "Steve, how do you like working from your new office?"

"It's great so far. The only thing I miss is Max jumping in my lap. My writer's block may be a thing of the past."

"That will solve your primary problem, but you still don't have a good writing coach or editor."

"I'll find one after we solve this case."

A thought came to her, but she didn't dare put words to it. That would be a task for another day or another year.

The server took orders for appetizers. Steve, Adam, and Bella chose raw oysters on the half-shell. This sparked the usual dualistic conversation, pitting lovers of the delicacies against those repulsed by the texture and taste. As always, no one changed their mind.

Conversation remained light throughout the meal, with no further mention of the murder they would investigate. Heather and Jack had settled into a routine where they'd take turns picking up the tab for meals. He presented his business credit card to the server and quipped, "Didn't we discuss a murder?"

"We certainly did," said Heather. "We talked about a family who may need the services of a gifted defense attorney. Someone like you."

"Good," said Jack. "I'll write this off as a business expense."

Rasheed spoke up. "Perhaps you tempt fate, my friend. Your reputation extends far and wide."

Heather and Jack looked at each other before she asked, "What if Rasheed is right and someone we investigate turns out to be the killer and they hire you to defend them?"

Jack countered with, "Houston is crawling with skilled attorneys. Why would they choose one from Conroe?"

Steve broke into their semi-private discussion. "You have to admit, that would be an interesting development."

The delivery and signing of the bill put an end to a meal that Heather thoroughly enjoyed. Their next stop would be at the historic Hotel Galvez, overlooking the sand and surf of the gulf. Tonight, they would dine with her father and the others. Tomorrow she'd board a cruise ship going to... "Jack, where is our ship going?"

"Does it matter?"

"Not really." A thought occurred to her. "In fact, don't tell me. I want to take life as it comes for a change."

Walking behind them, Steve said, "Good luck making that daydream a reality. You're not hard-wired to operate that way. You'll wake up early tomorrow morning and check messages on your phone while you're watching a business channel on television and reading *The Wall Street Journal*. Being on a cruise won't make much difference."

Jack responded before Heather could. "I think you're wrong, Steve. I'll wager a cheeseburger and fries that Heather can go cold-turkey from electronics from the time the ship gets underway until the end of the cruise."

"Why not see what she's really capable of? I think she should give up her phone before she boards the ship."

"I'm trying to be nice here. After all, we did spring this trip on her, so she hasn't had much time to prepare mentally."

"All right. I'll play nice this time."

After watching this exchange, Heather turned around and found Le Roi looking at her as if trying to tell her something. She ignored the dog and said, "Let's make the bet a little more interesting. Steve, I'll accept the bet that I can turn my phone off when the ship gets under way tomorrow and keep it off for the entire cruise. In fact, I'll up the ante and give it to Jack. You name the wager, but remember, it's you who's going to pay."

"You're on. And the wager is, whoever loses has to feed both dogs and Max for a week when you get back. Let's shake on it."

Le Roi picked that moment to fluff out his coat. Jack laughed out loud. "Le Roi sealed the bet for both of you."

Steve said, "I trained him to do that."

Heather thought he was joking, but wasn't sure enough to challenge him.

It wasn't long before they topped the I-45 bridge and looked down on Galveston Bay and the island city. That's when Steve's phone rang.

Between the road noise and the phone pressed hard against his ear, all she could hear was one side of the conversation.

"Hey, Leo," said Steve. "Did the park rangers get lucky and solve the case?" It seemed like minutes passed, but was probably only seconds, before Steve said, "That's interesting. How serious are the wounds?" ... "What hospital?" ... "Any witnesses?" ... "Where did it happen?" ... "Are you going to talk to her?" ... "We're almost there. Do you want me to?" ... "You're right. It can wait."

The call ended and Heather leaned forward. "I heard enough to know something important happened."

Steve spoke in a matter-of-fact tone. "Our victim's sister lives on Galveston Island. Someone beat her, slashed her with a knife, and shot her earlier today. She's at John Sealy Hospital getting patched up. Leo said the wounds aren't life threatening. No witnesses. She's not cooperating with the local police."

"That is interesting," said Jack.

Rasheed asked, "Steve, will you want to visit with the lady?"

"Not yet. Leo will find out what he can and let me know." He took off his sunglasses and rubbed his sightless eyes. "Heather, plan on you and Bella making a hospital visit tomorrow morning. I'd also like you, Jack, and your father to find out all you can about Stewart Clay. Come back from your cruise with a complete report."

"But I can't use my phone."

Steve brushed aside the excuse. "Use your father's satellite phone. We'll duplicate work, but we need to build a good foundation of knowledge before we interview people when you return."

# Chapter Nine

S teve waited in the kitchen for Rasheed to arrive the morning after he bid goodbye to those going on the cruise. Allister McBlythe, Heather's father, had insisted on treating them to supper. Under normal circumstances, Steve would have enjoyed the diversion, but it had been months since he'd challenged his mind with a murder to solve. His conversation had come out slow and garbled. At least, that's the way his words sounded to him. It had been a long time since he'd had to keep up a social conversation without letting on that his mind was elsewhere.

The sound of the garage door rolling up brought him off the barstool. He took his coffee cup to the sink, washed it, and double checked to make sure he'd turned off the coffeepot.

"Good morning, my friend," said Rasheed. It was his normal greeting but seemed brighter on this June day.

"You sound chipper," said Steve.

"A most descriptive word. It comes from the Northern English word *kipper*, which means nimble or frisky. It describes precisely how I feel today. What about you? Do you feel nimble or frisky?"

"Not yet. Perhaps some of your kipper will rub off on me."

"I recommend you exercise your mind by writing your story for an hour or more when we get to the office."

"Not a bad idea. What's on your schedule this morning?"

"Whatever you ask me to do."

Steve ran his tongue over his top front teeth as he searched for an answer. "I'd like for both of us to spend most of the day discovering what we can about Dan Clay and his sister Cindy. Both are victims. With Cindy in the hospital now after being attacked, we need to find out what we can about her also."

"Do you want me to focus on one and you on the other?"

"Not this time. We'll work separately on both, then compare notes. I told Heather to concentrate on Stewart Clay, our victim's father. When she returns, we'll have multiple reports. That way, nothing will fall through the cracks."

"That is one of the first idioms I learned when I was studying English as a child. There's no great mystery in its meaning, but you are wise to apply it to this investigation. I sense the solution is hiding in a tiny, easy-to-miss clue. Redundancy in our search is called for."

Steve sensed a spark of confidence ignite something within him. "Rasheed, let's get the dogs loaded in the car and go to work. If I go long periods without talking today, think nothing of it."

"There is great wisdom in exercising your mind more than your tongue."

"Did you make up that proverb?"

"I cannot take credit. I saw it on a YouTube video with many such sayings outside businesses and churches. There are many new proverbs in this country. Some are quite clever."

"I should have known," said Steve. "I'll grab my cane."

"Do you want me to keep Princess with me in my office this week?"

"That will be good. You can drop her off in my office if you need to go somewhere."

Steve felt Max rub against his leg. He bent down and gave the cat a head-to-tail series of strokes. "I've already fed you, old boy." The oversized cat's fur felt like sable.

"How old is Max?" asked Rasheed.

"I don't really know. He came as a package-deal with Heather."

"How did you two meet? I think my forgetter is working overtime, as you say."

"Allister insisted she leave police work and join him in running his business. He even had her fired from the Boston Police. She moved to Texas and tried to join Houston PD, but he pulled strings there, too.

"Her grandfather left her a ton of money, stocks, bonds, and who knows what else, but she couldn't access it until she turned thirty. I needed a partner to help me solve my friend's murder and she needed a refuge for a few months. I took her and Max in, and we worked our first case together. Max was full grown when they came." He thought for a moment. "I don't know how old he was when they moved in."

"His fur is mainly black, but gray is showing on his face."

"My barber tells me my hair and beard are gaining value by adding silver to the mix."

"Evidence of wisdom," said Rasheed.

Steve countered with, "Wisdom is the child of knowledge and hard work."

"I have never heard that proverb. Are there other children?"

"I know of four more. Wealth, health, and the twins, good and bad circumstances."

"Ah. You stretch my mind this morning."

"Good," said Steve. "Let's stick with knowledge and hard work today and see where they lead us."

The trip to the office passed mostly in silence as Steve mulled over the murder of Dan and the assault on his sister. The conversation and time spent meditating on what he already knew brought his thoughts into focus. Instead of writing a story of past exploits, he'd focus on the here and now. At least, that was his plan for the day.

Doris greeted them with an offer of coffee. "Not yet," said Steve. "I've done nothing to earn it yet." He considered explaining yesterday's events but opted to remain silent and work on the case.

Steve and Rasheed went to their offices, but both dogs stayed with Steve. The light floral fragrance of Doris's perfume followed him into the room. He heard the door shut behind her. "Heather called and wanted me to tell you not to call her until after lunch. Her ship won't sail until five this afternoon."

Steve propped his cane against the side of a file cabinet and felt his way around his desk and into his chair. "Did she say why I shouldn't call before noon?"

"She told me she and Bella are going to the hospital to visit the daughter of an old friend of her father's."

"Thanks. We briefly discussed that yesterday. I wasn't sure if they had time to go or not."

"Is there anything else you need?"

"Not for a couple of hours. Then, I'll need the winner of today's lottery to take Le Roi and Princess outside."

"Two winners," said Doris. "After the great chase I decided two handlers would be better than one."

"Excellent decision."

Footfalls headed to the door, and it clicked shut once Doris reached the hallway. Steve spoke to the furry occupants. "It's time for me to get to work. Princess, I have a feeling your mom stayed up very late last night doing research on Cindy Clay before their hospital visit today."

———

THE SERVER FILLED cups of coffee for Heather and her father in the Monarch Dining Room, within Hotel Galvez. They'd stayed up late doing research, and neither had much of an appetite. Heather chose a cup of fruit while her father followed her lead but added a croissant. Heather couldn't get over how different her father looked wearing loose-fitting tan slacks, a white linen Mexican wedding shirt, and brown leather boat shoes with no socks. All he needed was to put on the straw Panama hat he'd brought, and he'd be ready to sail.

Heather matched his casual look with a simple floral-print romper and white sandals. She looked over her raised cup and asked, "How did you sleep?"

He let out a little groan. "Not as good as I'm going to sleep tonight. The older I get, the more I enjoy getting away from the office and home. I wasn't counting on staying awake until the wee hours doing last-minute research on Stewart Clay." He took a sip of coffee. "How late were you up?"

She spoke through a yawn. "My watch tracks my sleep, and it was two-fifteen when my breathing and heart rate declined."

"What did you discover about Cindy Clay?"

Heather took another, longer sip and rested her cup on the table. "She's nothing like her late brother, perhaps because she came along seventeen years after Daniel. By the way, he went by the abbreviated version of his name, Dan."

"That pregnancy must have been a surprise to her parents." A wistful look of remembrance came over his face. "I've never told you this, but your mother and I had a similar experience.

There were ten years between you and the first child your mother miscarried."

Heather felt her heart flutter. This was news to her. "Was it a boy or a girl?"

Her father brought sad eyes to bear on her. "Your mother didn't want to tell me. We'd only been married four months when she conceived."

Heather considered the revelation. "She didn't want to tell you because it was a boy. You lost the son you always wanted."

"We lost that child, but God blessed us with another."

Heather reached out her hand and placed it on her father's. "I can't imagine how hard it must have been for you and Mother."

"I'm afraid we didn't handle it well. I fought my pain with incessant work. Your mother battled the loss by getting involved in charities and civic and social organizations. We thought we'd never have another child."

"And when you did, you feared the worst until I was born." She thought, but didn't dare say for fear of upsetting them both, that she wasn't the boy he had longed for. She cleared her throat and squared her shoulders. "Thank you for telling me, Dad, but let's not dwell on the past." To get them on lighter ground, she grinned and joked, "Besides, we have other things to think about. Steve and I may have a murder and an attempted murder to solve."

Allister gave a slight smile. "You're right. Are you sure Dan's death is a murder?"

"Steve is, and that's good enough for me."

She looked at her coffee cup but didn't raise it. "This discussion of the age difference between Dan and Cindy Clay helps me understand why they are so different. It's not only that they were so many years apart, but they had absolutely nothing in common."

71

"Nothing?"

"The only thing they shared was the same father and mother." She stopped as a thought exploded in her mind. "Perhaps I should say the same father appears on both their birth certificates. That may not mean he sired both."

"You sound like a detective, always looking at possibilities."

Heather considered his statement. "True, but it's also true that most possibilities lead to dead ends. I have no reason to believe they were half-siblings."

She took a big breath and regrouped. "After Stewart's wife died, he married a much younger woman named Lisa Roberts."

"I vaguely remember Stewart's first wife, but I've never met his current wife. His first wife's name was Patricia. Lung cancer claimed her when Cindy was a child." He then asked, "How old is Cindy now?"

"Twenty-four, with a degree in environmental studies."

"That would put her brother Dan at forty-one."

"Correct," said Heather. "And the patriarch, Stewart Clay, is in his mid-sixties. The stepmother, Lisa Roberts-Clay, is thirty-seven."

"Not surprising," said her father. "Wealthy men have a habit of picking young, attractive women after losing their first spouse."

The server came back with their breakfast choices and warmed their coffee. Jack, Adam, and Bella joined them and ordered coffee.

"No breakfast?" asked Heather.

"I'm still stuffed from last night," said Bella.

"Coffee first," said Jack and Adam at the same time.

Heather then asked Bella, "When are you planning to leave for home?"

Bella looked at Adam, who shrugged. "After you two get back from the hospital."

"Do you and Dad want to go with us?" asked Heather.

Allister shook his head. "You two go. Cindy may be more talkative if two beautiful women come to her room."

"Good idea," said Jack. "I'm in vacation mode and a few laps in the pool sounds like a good way to start the day."

Adam added, "I'll take a quick peek at the markets then join you."

"Me, too," said her father.

Heather looked at Bella. "I'm ready when you are."

The two women rose and left the men to drink coffee and whatever else they wanted to do.

The trip across the long narrow island only lasted a few minutes. The medical complex of buildings included the University of Texas Medical School, John Sealy Hospital, and the newer thirteen-story addition. It took asking for directions twice before they found Cindy's room.

Heather tapped on the door before entering, with Bella acting as her shadow. "Good morning," said Heather.

"Uh. Who are you?" asked the woman in a soft voice. She reminded Heather of a field mouse with a weak chin and a nose that was half a size too large for her face. Her long, straight hair was the color of Galveston's brownish sand.

"My name is Heather McBlythe, and this is Bella Webber."

Bella smiled at the young woman who was pulling the sheet up higher. "Hello, Cindy. We stopped in to see how you're feeling today."

The young woman stared at Bella. "You look familiar. Are you famous?"

Bella moved closer. "You might have seen me on television, or the movie they made of my life. A man named Brumley kidnapped me and raised me as his daughter. He had a hunting show on television and used me to show a softer side to the sport. After he died, I stopped hunting and took up fishing for a while. Catch and release only. Now I model outdoor clothing."

Heather saw the woman's grip on the sheet relax. "I remember your fishing show. You were the most beautiful girl I'd ever seen, and I dreamed of going to the places you fished. Now that I see you in person, you're even more perfect." She looked away, a pink flush staining her cheeks. "I'm glad you stopped hunting and fishing. I love animals. Dogs and cats are my thing."

Wanting to keep the woman at ease, Heather broke into the conversation. "You'd love my cat, Max, and my dog Princess. Max is the biggest, most lovable Maine coon you've ever seen. He's extra-large and sleeps with me every night. Princess is my support dog."

Bella confirmed Heather's comments with a firm nod. "They're both extra special."

"Do you two visit people in the hospital often?" asked Cindy.

"Not as much as I'd like to." Bella took her hand. "How are you feeling?"

Heather thought about taking over the interview, but Bella had already formed a bond, so she stood back.

"Pretty good. The doctors said I'll go home tomorrow unless the shrink says I should stay." She broke eye contact. "Someone beat me up, cut my arm, and shot me."

"That's terrible," said Bella. "Did they rob you?"

"No. I guess they got scared."

Heather asked, "Did this happen in Galveston?"

Cindy avoided eye contact. "Uh-huh. In the condo I share with a friend. She wasn't home."

"I see the bandage on your shoulder and the black eye," said Bella. "Did you say they shot you, too?"

Pointing to a spot under the sheet, she explained. "It was a small caliber bullet, and it went in and out of my left cheek. The doctor said the angle was perfect for not leaving much of a scar. It didn't hit anything important."

Bella said, "You and I have something in common. I have a similar scar on my right side, thanks to a small shark who thought my backside looked like a tasty snack."

The door flew open and a woman with a crewcut hairstyle walked in. "Who are you, and why are you talking to Cindy?"

Bella released Cindy's hand. "Hello. My name is Bella Webber. Cindy and I were trading stories of scars we both have on our backside."

Cindy tried to explain. "I used to watch Bella on television. Fishing shows."

Heather interrupted. "My name is Heather. I didn't catch yours."

"That's because it's none of your business." The woman yanked open the door and said with barely restrained fury, "Get out."

Heather turned to face Cindy. "Do you want us to go?"

Fear shone in Cindy's eyes. "Yes, please."

Heather shifted her gaze to the other woman. "We're leaving because Cindy asked us politely. You should try it sometime."

Heather took out her phone and snapped a photo of the woman.

"You can't take my picture!"

"Who says I can't?"

"Me and the law."

Heather laughed. "Silly woman. I'm an attorney and idle threats from someone who doesn't know what they're talking about mean nothing to me." She turned to Cindy. "I hope you have a full and speedy recovery."

The unknown woman's voice echoed in the hall despite the closed door to Cindy's room.

"That didn't end the way I thought it would," said Bella.

"Did you notice the words on the T-shirt she was wearing?"

"Something about the planet."

"It read: *Kill Big Oil Before It Kills The Planet.*"

# Chapter Ten

S teve's phone chimed and identified the caller as Heather. "Are you on board the ship yet?"

"We are. The captain arranged for us to have the red-carpet treatment from the time we arrived at the cruise terminal. We're all in our suites, freshening up before lunch."

"I sent out for a sandwich," said Steve with a pitiful tone to his words.

"Poor thing. You should have come with us."

"Work comes before play. You, of all people, should know that." He took a hurried breath. "And speaking of work, how did your interview with Cindy Clay go?"

"She wasn't anything like I thought she'd be. She cowers at the sight of her own shadow."

"That's similar to what Bella said. She called and gave me a report on the meeting. I'm curious about the human guard dog who threw you out of Cindy's room."

"I found no redeeming qualities in that woman. One-hundred percent bully. It wouldn't surprise me if she's the one who put Cindy in the hospital. She exhibited all the signs of a battered woman."

Steve took his turn again. "Bella told me you took a photo of the woman."

"I sent it to Bella with instructions to do a full background check on her."

"Bella told me about that, too. She worked on it on the drive through Houston. The woman's name is Claire Strobel. Her chief claim to fame is multiple arrests for destructive environmental protests against oil companies. Leo's running a rap sheet for us."

Heather asked, "Is she destructive enough for the FBI to have a file on her?"

"I don't know. You can check on that, too, but there's no rush. I'm sure you'll have plenty of time between playing bingo, going to shows, and stuffing yourself with prime rib and lobster."

"You forgot to mention spin classes, yoga, massages, and the spa treatments I plan on fitting into my schedule."

A few seconds passed before Heather said, "It might be a good idea if I check with my buddy at the CIA. Claire impressed me as the type of person who'd stop at nothing if it helped her cause."

"Good idea, and don't forget to include your father. I'd like a full report on Stewart Clay, his late wife Patricia, and his current wife Lisa. Like I said, no rush. Anytime in the next day or two will be fine," he said tongue-in-cheek.

Heather released a huff. "I thought this was supposed to be a pleasure cruise."

"It is. You derive pleasure from working cases. So does everyone else except Jack."

Heather let out a humorless chuckle. "Jack has his own set

of worries to keep him busy. The friend Briann brought along is keeping Jack and his mother on their toes."

"Oh? How so?"

"She's what you might call an early bloomer and fills out a bathing suit better than most Hollywood actresses. Last night, the girls ate early then went to the hotel pool. They didn't lack for company, especially Cammy."

"Are they in a stateroom by themselves?"

"There's an adjoining door between Jack's room and theirs. Briann's not crazy about Jack making them keep it open. If it was Briann by herself, she wouldn't mind. According to Jack, Cammy wouldn't have been his first choice of girls to bring along."

"I wouldn't worry about Briann. She'll tire of a friend like that pretty soon. Briann is too much like you," said Steve.

"What do you mean by that wise crack?"

"You both love to work. And she's focused. Briann can't wait to become an attorney like you."

"Don't you mean like her late mother?"

"Her, too."

Silence took over for a couple of seconds before Steve asked, "How's Jack's mother enjoying her trip so far?"

"So far, so good. She and my father seem to enjoy each other's company. I hadn't thought about it, but everyone has someone their own age to talk to on this trip. Thank you again for arranging this."

Instead of coming up with a snappy response, Steve spoke a simple, "You're welcome."

Heather moved on. "What does the rest of your day look like?"

"I'll eat my sandwich, take the dogs downstairs to sniff around, and wait for Adam to drop Bella off. We'll keep working on background information. I'm expecting to find a few loose strings to pull to see where they lead."

"More suspects?"

"Oil executives have a habit of making enemies. I'm counting on you and your father to find at least one or two. Rasheed, Bella, and I will look for others."

"I can take a hint. Good hunting."

"Same to you, and bon voyage."

The phone went silent. He hoped Heather would enjoy the sail-away party today and turn loose of some of her fortune in the ship's spa.

A knock on his door sounded, and he hollered, "Come in, Rasheed."

The door's top hinge had an almost imperceptible squeak as the man of many talents came in. "Are you ready to break for lunch?"

"Yes, such as it is. Unlike some people we know, I am having a working man's fare for lunch."

"Ah. You spoke to Heather. I thought I heard you talking on the phone."

Steve picked up the office phone and punched in a number. Pam, Heather's personal assistant, answered. "Are the puppies ready for lunch?"

"We all are. I can come get their food if you're busy."

"No need. Their steaks came cut into cubes. I'll be down with their bowls before you can punch the call button for the elevator."

"Thank you. I just spoke with Heather. She didn't ask about how things are going here."

"That's cause for celebration. I'll bring you a soft drink."

"Bring one for yourself and one for Rasheed."

Steve felt with his right hand and placed the phone back in its cradle with his left. He hadn't made enough calls to know the phone's exact location on his desk. A couple more times and he'd have it committed to memory.

He leaned back. "What have you done this morning?"

Rasheed shifted in his chair. "The most significant accomplishment was to speak with Junani again."

"How is the overqualified attorney today?"

"You speak words that are daggers in my heart. I fear she is exactly as you say, overqualified. Too perfect to be a mere mortal."

Steve interlaced his fingers and rested his hands on his desk. "I thought that about my wife on our first couple of dates. By the end of our third one, I knew she was something even better—a mortal who thought I was special."

"What made you believe she wasn't a goddess?"

"She took a big drink of fizzy cola and sneezed before swallowing. It splattered all over me and the inside of my car. After that, every time either of us sneezed, we'd look at each other and smile."

Rasheed gave his head a firm nod. "A simple story about a shared memory of two lovers. You're right. Gods and goddesses are not very good at laughing about their weaknesses. From now on, I'll picture Junani spraying cola from her mouth and nose."

Steve wagged his head. "It doesn't work when you try to borrow a memory. You'll have to make your own. Be yourself and allow her to be herself. It won't take long before one of you proves you have feet of clay."

"Ah! An idiom from the Bible, the book of Daniel. It speaks of a hidden physical weakness or a flaw in the character of a highly respected person." He rubbed his chin. "You are most wise, Steve."

Another knock on the door brought both dogs to their feet. Pam entered and presented Le Roi and Princess with their meals of raw steak. Le Roi sniffed his for freshness before making quick work of devouring it. Princess didn't hesitate to dig in but savored the meal at a more leisurely pace.

Doris joined the gathering with sandwiches and chips for Steve and Rasheed. Pam announced, "Steve, your soft drink is at 10 o'clock."

"I hope he doesn't sneeze," said Rasheed.

Steve chuckled. "Don't pay attention to us. It's an inside joke about something that happened a long time ago."

He opened the bag of potato chips, took a bite of one, and waited until he swallowed to say, "This tastes like a shrimp cocktail."

"I don't understand," said Rasheed.

"Never mind," said Steve. "It's something I told Heather I'd say when I ate a potato chip for lunch while she's dining on a real shrimp cocktail."

"Why would you say that?" asked Rasheed.

"The answer will come to you later. The western sense of humor sometimes evades you."

"Speaking of Heather," said Pam. "We're still on schedule to have you and Heather moved."

Steve had taken a rather large bite from his sandwich, forcing him to nod his head instead of responding with words. He finally swallowed and said, "Thank you so much for staying on top of things while Heather's gone. I'm convinced she has the best employees in the world."

"She's the type of woman that makes us want to do better than our best," said Pam. "I need to get back to work or she'll dock my pay."

"Me, too," said Doris. "Enjoy the rest of your lunch. I'll send the next two lucky winners to take the king and princess outside."

Le Roi responded with a soft whimper of agreement.

Steve and Rasheed had just finished their meal when Steve's phone rang and announced Leo as the caller.

"What's new?" asked Steve.

"Did I interrupt you eating a steak?"

"Only the dogs get food like that. Did you call to give me good news?"

"It's news, but it's not good. Stewart Clay is raising a ruckus about the death of his son. There's still not an official ruling on his death and he's fit to be tied."

Rasheed mumbled, "I wonder what the origin of the word *ruckus* is."

Steve ignored the former professor and asked, "Other than being angry, what's Mr. Clay done?"

"He's called the mayors of La Porte, Pasadena, Baytown, Galveston, and Houston. He's also called the governor, the head of the Department of Public Safety, as well as the top man over the state park police. That gentleman received a special dressing down from Mr. Clay. But that's nothing compared to what he said to the coroner."

"Are you feeling the heat yet?"

"Not directly, but I'm treading lightly. If word gets out that I went to the crime scene with you and Heather, my name may go on Stewart Clay's naughty list."

Steve spoke with confidence. "You worry too much. That's a long list and you're nowhere near the top."

"Not yet, but there's more."

This comment made Steve sit up straight. "Keep talking, Leo."

"The victim, Dan Clay, was a city councilman. Daddy's money got him there."

"So? Big money and Houston politics go together like peanut butter and jelly."

"Do you remember a former city councilman named Leonard Spears?"

"I remember his enforcer, Bill Boyd, better. You and I sent him to Huntsville for thirty-five years on a murder with a deadly weapon charge. Spears spent a load of money to make sure Boyd didn't get life."

"He kept spending money after you had to retire. Last year, the courts overturned the case because of a faulty indictment from the DA's office."

Steve put the pieces together. "I think I know where you're going with this. Spears is a man of dubious character who sponsored a man to take care of problems with his businesses and with his political foes. His enforcer got sloppy, earned a one-way trip to the state prison, but is now out."

"Exactly," said Leo. "Word on the street is that Leonard Spears holds grudges for a long time. There's been bad blood between Spears and Stewart Clay ever since the election that put Dan Clay on the city council."

Steve took over. "And now Bill Boyd, Leonard Spears's enforcer, is out of prison and working for Spears again. How loud is Stewart Clay screaming that Spears is responsible for his son's death?"

Leo hollered at someone to get his feet off their desk before saying, "Turn on the news tonight and you'll hear for yourself."

"What precautions is Spears taking?"

"His home is already a fortress. Bill Boyd is his top man. I'm not sure how many others he's hired."

Steve caught himself nodding, stopped, and asked, "What about Stewart Clay? Has he beefed up protection?"

"Another fortress, but this one is in River Oaks. Tall iron fences with only one gate, security cameras, and armed guards with dogs."

Steve spoke mainly to himself. "This could get out of hand fast."

"Tell me about it," said Leo. "Both men have way too much money and pride. Once the shooting starts, it might not end until the morgue puts out a No Vacancy sign."

Again, Steve spoke mainly to himself. "I need to get Stewart Clay to hire me and Heather." Then he raised his voice a decibel and said, "It would be best if you and the boys in blue stay out of this as long as you can. Too much possibility of collateral damage."

Steve took a full breath and held it for several seconds before releasing it. "Let me think about how I can get hired. There's an idea rolling around in my head."

# Chapter Eleven

Heather finished her morning workout, wrapped a towel around her neck, and went to her father's penthouse cabin. It reminded her of a luxury apartment with two bedrooms, two full bathrooms, a kitchen, living and dining rooms, and a private balcony. Located on the upper deck, floor to ceiling glass in the living room gave views that reached out to where sky met water.

"Nice digs," said Heather.

Her father shrugged. "Someone must have heard I'm considering selling half my stock. I reserved a standard balcony room." He made a sweeping motion with his hand. "Not this. However, there is one perk you might enjoy. Would you like a fruit smoothie?"

"That would be wonderful."

Allister picked up the receiver of a red phone. "George, I need a strawberry and mango smoothie as soon as possible."

Heather chuckled. "I take it George is your butler."

"They call him a personal concierge. I watch what I say around him. In fact, I need to be more discreet talking about my travel plans here than around the office in Boston." He tilted his head. "Do you have trouble with spies?"

"Not much. Steve helps me set traps for them. He says all he does is think like someone who has a weak moral compass."

"Interesting," said her father. "Are you saying he thinks like a thief?"

"Thief, pickpocket, swindler, spurned lover, paid informer, extortionist, killer, you name it, and he can put himself in almost anyone's shoes."

"Fascinating." Her father looked away then brought his gaze back to her. "What about you? Can you take on a different persona so you think like a criminal?"

"Not like Steve unless I'm wearing a convincing disguise. He does it all in his mind. I need props."

A knock on the door put the discussion on hold. Since she was closest to the door, she opened it, then stood back as a rather swarthy looking man entered. After an initial glimpse at her, he gave a perfunctory, shallow bow, averted his eyes, and walked to within five feet of her father before asking, "Where would you like this placed?"

Heather followed him and spoke before her father could. "I'll take it, George." She lifted it from a silver tray.

"As you wish, ma'am."

Heather said, "Your face is familiar, George. Have we ever met?"

"That's a remote possibility, Ms. McBlythe."

"No, there's something about you that's ringing a bell. Did you ever live in New York?"

"I'm a Londoner, born and raised," he said in a stiff British accent.

"You must be chuffed to have a job on this ship."

"Uh... of course."

He quickly shifted his gaze to her father. "May I be of further service to you, Mr. McBlythe?"

"Do you want breakfast, Heather?"

"Not now, thank you."

"That's all for now, George," said her father.

The door shut and Heather looked up at her father as he gave her a knowing look and said, "You tested him. Did you really recognize him?"

"No, but I made him think I did."

"Why did you choose New York?"

"The large number of theaters. He's an actor, or he was at one time. Did you notice how quickly he claimed to be from London? He didn't want to talk about New York."

A smile of satisfaction came across her father's face. "He certainly wasn't London born and raised. He didn't know that the slang word *chuffed* meant very happy."

The smile on her father's face left him. "If George is no longer an actor, and he's not an English butler, what is he? A spy?"

"It's more likely he's a former actor and current private detective hired for this voyage only. I can find out if you want me to, but there's a better way to handle this if you decide to sell a good portion of your stock."

"What do you propose?"

"Keep doing what you're doing and enjoy the cruise. On the day before the cruise ends, write a positive report and hint that you might be interested in purchasing additional stock."

Allister put the pieces together in his mind. "If you're right about George, or whatever his name is, the price of the stock shouldn't go down before I can sell it."

He rubbed his hands together. "I see what you mean about thinking like a crook. You're actually very good at it and you didn't wear a costume."

"No, but George did."

Heather sipped her smoothie, walked to the window, and looked out on a blue sky dotted sparsely with clouds floating across it like puffy balls of cotton.

Her father's voice sounded from over her shoulder. "Do you want to call Steve and see how things are progressing with the murder case?"

"Let's wait until this afternoon. Jack and I will hand the girls over to his mother, and he'll want to hear what Steve has to say."

"Isn't there a club for teens on this ship?"

Heather nodded. "Jack said Briann is good with it, but her friend thinks it's too juvenile. She's pressuring Briann to spend the day by the pools."

"They'll be red as lobsters if they spend too much time in the sun." He considered what he just said. "I sound like your mother."

Heather didn't argue. "I can still hear her saying those same words. I'll make sure they slather on the sunblock this morning."

After trading kisses on the cheek, Heather left her father and his satellite phone. His idea of a restful trip was to call his department managers and move a chess piece or two in the game of high finance.

She returned to her cabin and took a warm shower. The hair dryer hanging on the wall worked well enough to do the job. The previous week, she'd taken two inches off the length, but her auburn locks still reached halfway down her back. After applying a dab or two of makeup around the eyes, the laugh lines all but disappeared.

The stray thought of Steve taking care of two dogs and a cat floated through her mind, but took flight when the phone in her room rang. Jack's voice came through loud and clear. "I don't know about you, but I'm ready for breakfast."

Heather responded with, "Main dining room, buffet, or the little cafe with specialty coffee and pastries?" Before he could answer, she asked, "Where do the girls want to go?"

"They already left for the buffet."

"That makes sense," said Heather with teasing in her voice. "Better chance of seeing boys there."

Jack moaned. "Don't remind me. It's room service for Mom this morning."

"That's what my dad will do. I stopped in to see him after sunrise yoga and a few miles on the treadmill."

"Have you heard from Steve?"

"Not yet. I thought I'd wait until this afternoon."

"Good call. It's not been a full day since you spoke to him. What could have happened in that amount of time?"

Heather countered the question with a firm reply. "Plenty. Don't underestimate his ability to stir up a hornet's nest."

Jack's stomach must have objected to the conversation. 'Instead of talking on the phone like a couple of pimply-faced teens, let's go to the buffet and enjoy a breakfast of copious amounts of fried meats, pancakes, pastries, and other fattening foods."

"That was almost enough to ruin my appetite. I'll meet you in the hall."

Heather insisted they take the stairs. To his credit, Jack took moderate servings and refrained from all but one waffle. They located the girls, who were finishing their meals. Briann did the talking. "Is it all right if we change and go to the pool?"

"Isn't it a little early?" asked Jack. "Other activities start in half an hour. Did you check the day's itinerary on the television and make a plan?"

Cammy scrunched her nose in a way that left no doubt she

didn't approve of the suggestion. Briann had a more complete answer. "I took a quick look at it. Other than the teen club and the activities by the pool, nothing appealed to me. We're not really into newlywed game show or trivia."

Heather broke in. "Would you rather swim this morning or this afternoon?"

"Both," said Cammy, without hesitation.

Jack shook his head. "There's hardly a cloud in the sky. You'll cook if you spend all day in the sun."

"There's plenty of shady spots and we'll wear gobs of sunscreen. My mom made me bring two tubes."

Jack held up his palms as a sign of surrender. "Heather and I will come check on you in an hour."

"Perhaps sooner," said Heather. "I wouldn't mind baking in the sun for half an hour while reading the book I brought."

The morning passed without incident as the girls stayed mostly in the shade but made occasional trips into one of the hot tubs or pools. Their appetites came alive a few minutes before noon and the group retired to their respective rooms to change for lunch. Jack's mother joined them for lunch at the buffet.

Jack filled a plate with an assortment of salads. His mother, Cora, gave him a sideways glance. "Is that all you're having?"

"I was too lazy to get up and exercise with Heather this morning. After a full breakfast, I need to pace myself on eating or someone might put a harpoon in me."

Cora shifted her gaze. "Heather, will your father join us?"

"I called him when we returned from swimming. He's dealing with a minor crisis at his office in Boston."

"I hope it's nothing too serious."

"Nothing that a pink slip and severance pay won't fix. Only one employee this time."

"You make it sound common."

She tilted her head. "Letting people go is not an everyday occurrence, but it's not uncommon either. It's surprising what people do to get fired. It's almost like they want someone to release them from the burden of doing the job they spent so much effort getting."

Jack tapped his temple with an index finger. "I think it's caused by worms in the brain."

Heather rolled her eyes and changed the subject. "You and I can check on Dad while your mom takes over chaperone duties."

"We'll start with a nap after lunch," said Cora as she stood to leave. "Tropical sun will not only burn you, it has a sedative effect. There will be more than enough time for them to swim this afternoon."

The knock on her father's door brought a quick, stiff response from George, the butler. "Please come in, Ms. McBlythe and Mr. Blackwood. May I get you something to eat or drink?"

"A glass of water with ice for me," said Heather as she walked past him.

"Make it two," said Jack. "Straight. No chaser."

George chuckled.

Jack walked to the windows and let out a low whistle. "Nice view if you like water and sky. I'm not sure how I would like it in a hurricane or if I spotted a waterspout."

"You have four choices when that happens," said Allister with mischief in his voice. "You can draw the curtains and put on a sleep mask, then pretend you're riding a roller coaster with nothing to restrain you."

This earned a chuckle from Jack, but Heather had heard the options many times. "Go on, Dad, finish them. We have things to discuss."

Allister cleared his throat. "The second option is to lash

yourself to something bolted down, leave the curtains open, and ride out the storm like a true sailor."

Jack shook his head. "That would be messy when seasickness hit. Let's hear option three."

"If seasickness is an issue, immediately leave the penthouse, find the lowest midpoint of the ship, and stay there until the storm passes."

"I'd be afraid the ship would capsize, and I'd be back at the top of the ship, riding a roller coaster upside down. What's the last option?"

"Sneak onto a lifeboat and hope for the best."

Jack rubbed his chin. "I'd take option one. I love a good roller coaster."

Heather joined him at the window. "Next you'll be telling me you want to do the big water slide that goes from the top deck, out over the water, and empties onto the main deck."

"It's on my bucket list. What about it? Are you up for a thrill this afternoon?"

George approached with glasses on a tray. Heather kept looking out the window but said, "Just put those on the coffee table."

He did as instructed and asked, "Is there anything else I can do for you, Mr. McBlythe?"

"That's all, George. I'll call if I need you."

The click of the door was Heather's signal to face her father. "I'd like to call Steve and get an update on the case."

"Let's go to the dining room table. I have a preliminary report to share concerning Stewart Clay."

# Chapter Twelve

B ella and Adam arrived in Steve's office a few minutes before his phone rang. Le Roi and Princess were taking their afternoon naps but rose to greet their future neighbors with tails wagging. Steve had yet to find a dog or cat that didn't fall under Bella's spell within minutes of her fawning over them.

His phone spoke the name Allister McBlythe.

"Good afternoon, Allister," said Steve. "How's the weather?"

"Smooth as glass. We'll dock in Montego Bay tomorrow morning, and on to the Cayman Islands the next day. Do you want me to give you my report first?"

"How long is it?"

"Not long. It's mainly a financial report on Stewart Clay."

"Can you summarize it for us?"

Heather jumped in. "Who's us?"

"Hello, my long-lost shipmate. Us includes me, Bella, Adam, Rasheed, and two sleepy dogs."

The sound of Heather's voice brought Princess to her feet and Steve heard a soft whimper.

Steve corrected his most recent words. "Make that one sleepy dog. You-know-who misses her mother."

Allister took over again. "Stewart Clay has done well for himself in the oil business. Shrewd foreign acquisitions in the last few years have moved him from seven figures to eight. He mostly plays by the rules, but there are plenty who say he's not above stretching them until they scream. He tries to keep a low profile unless it comes to philanthropy. Even then, he pushes his current wife ahead of him and into the limelight. Her name is Lisa Roberts-Clay. Most of the time she uses her maiden name to minimize his exposure."

"What about enemies?"

"There's no shortage of those, and they fall into two categories. The first relates to business dealings with people who believe they wound up on the wrong side of a deal." He paused. "*Enemy* is probably too strong of a word to describe them. Rapidly aging children with bruised egos is better. The second group includes local, national and international organizations dedicated to the elimination of fossil fuels."

"Who stands out with those groups?"

"That's hard to say because there are so many of them. There's enough evidence to suggest a cabal of wealthy people, as well as various countries, direct the protests. Under them, there's what you could call officers of various ranks. Under them are the foot soldiers who do the protesting. Most are peaceful, but there's always some who take things too far."

Allister kept talking. "I also found something that pertained specifically to Stewart Clay's son. It seems Dan Clay dethroned a man named Leonard Spears from his seat on the city council."

"Yes, Leo and I discussed the event. In fact, I was involved in sending a man to prison for a murder related to that election."

Heather interrupted. "I don't remember hearing that story."

"It was a simple case that was open and shut. A guy named Bill Boyd took a shot at Dan Clay, missed him, but hit his campaign manager. Cameras caught the shooting, and Leo and I tracked the guy down before he boarded a chartered plane for Mexico."

"How much time did he get?"

"Thirty-five years, aggravated."

"That's a relief. He won't be out for a long time."

Steve hesitated, wondering if he should tell her the rest of the story. He concluded Heather would find out whether he told her or not. "Um... about that prison sentence. It seems the court of criminal appeals found something wrong with the original indictment and the guy who killed the campaign manager is back in Houston, working for Leonard Spears again."

"Mmmm," was all Steve heard from Heather. He expected more of an explosion, but it didn't come. A bad guy getting off lightly normally triggered her sense of justice, which in turn caused her Boston politeness to go by the wayside. He waded back into the conversation with trepidation. "Boyd is bad news. He made sure Leonard Spears received full, on-time payments for any products sold or monies borrowed. Legal or otherwise."

"I understand," said Heather. "He's Leonard Spears's heavy."

"Rasheed appreciates your choice of words. I'd like for you to do something for me."

His voice took on a tone she'd heard many times before... all business with not a pinch of frustration. "Yes? What is it?"

"Leo believes the lid is about to blow off the feud between Stewart Clay and Leonard Spears. Both men are turning their homes into armed fortresses. So far, it's only a battle of words.

Revenge is in the air, as thick as low-grade oil. It's only a matter of time before someone does something stupid."

"I understand the problem, but I'm stuck on this ship."

"Your brain still works, doesn't it?"

"Most of the time, but—"

He cut her off. "I want you, your dad, and Jack to come up with a plan to get me an appointment to talk to Stewart Clay. If I can convince him to give us time to find the person or persons who killed his son, we might avoid a real mess."

"What if we discover that Leonard Spears and his henchman killed him?"

"Then Leo or the park police, or whoever wants the credit, takes our evidence and arrests them."

"And if it's someone else not related to or hired by either Clay or Spears?"

"Then there's a chance Leonard Spears goes back to hating Stewart Clay without resorting to violence."

"Or," said Heather, "we could let the police do their job."

"If you were here and not aboard a floating city heading for Jamaica, you wouldn't say that."

Heather released a huff. "I want you to promise me you won't do anything stupid before I get home. You have a history with the guy who killed our victim's campaign manager. There's a good possibility he corrected his mistake and killed Dan Clay. I have a bad feeling he remembers you."

"I'm sure he does. That's why I only want to meet with Stewart Clay until you get back."

He rethought his last words. "There may be one or two of Clay's family that Bella could have a chance encounter with."

Heather let out a huff of frustration. "Don't you dare put her in danger. That goes for Adam and Rasheed, too."

Steve smiled. "I was only thinking out loud."

"Try selling that load of fertilizer to someone else. I'm not buying it. You've been stagnant too long and you're itching to do whatever it takes to find who killed Dan Clay."

"You know me too well."

"Do I have your word that you won't conduct any interviews until I'm home?"

"Not unless Leo goes with me. He's keeping a low profile, so there's not much chance of me crossing the county line."

"It's a deal," said Heather. "I'll do what I can from here. You stay in Montgomery County."

Steve asked, "Is there anything else we need to discuss before you get back to fun and frolic?"

Jack had a ready answer. "Something tells me this cruise won't be as restful as we planned. Heather now has the look of a huntress in her eyes."

"Sorry for the bad timing," said Steve. "Killers have a habit of committing their homicides at the most inconvenient times for us."

"Is there anything else?" asked Allister.

"Use the highest SPF number sunscreen you can find," said Bella. "Nothing ruins a vacation like a bad sunburn."

"Thanks, Bella. That's all from here," said Steve. "I'll call if a significant development occurs before you get home."

Allister closed the conversation with, "We'll spend the afternoon thinking of ways to get you and Heather an interview with Stewart Clay."

———————

HEATHER AND JACK spent the first hour after the phone call in the specialty cafe drinking designer coffee with an extra shot of espresso. To further stimulate their brains, they shared a huge cream-filled pastry with chocolate icing. The sugar and caffeine had them buzzing to the point they had to go to the promenade deck and walk laps around the ship.

Jack spoke as they set off at a quick pace. "Perhaps it wasn't such a good idea to come on this cruise."

"The idea was perfect, and I love everyone for trying to help me complete my recovery. Like Steve said, it's lousy timing. But there was no way to know about this case when you planned it."

Jack looked out to sea. "It's not only the timing, I included too many people."

"What do you mean?"

"It should have been just you and your dad. You could have helped him decide on the stock sale in half the time. You know as well as I do, he's grooming you to take over his companies."

A counter to Jack's words rose in her, but she tamped it down and kept walking. "You have a valid point, but he values your opinion, too."

Jack jerked his gaze away from the horizon. "You and your father play in the major leagues with business deals. I'm content to play on a much smaller field." He gave her a smile. "That doesn't mean I'm not a darn good defense attorney—there's nothing wrong with my self-esteem."

She took his hand. "There's nothing wrong with the rest of you, either."

"If you're trying to win my heart, you succeeded a long time ago."

He squeezed her hand. "Let's get back to my poor timing. I should have known that you and Steve were overdue for working a case. There's a strange rhythm to that side of the two of you. Most people go on vacations to recharge. You and Steve solve murders."

Heather wrapped her arm around his waist and kept walking.

"You're right again. The interview Bella and I started with Cindy Clay lit a fire in me I can't put out. All I can think about is interviewing her again without that Strobel woman intimidating her."

Jack walked a little slower. "I noticed a couple of other things that tell me we aren't where we're supposed to be. Briann chose the wrong girl to bring with her."

Heather jumped in. "Your little girl may be a teen, but she's not comfortable with her womanhood yet. She has a moral compass that doesn't stray from due north." She paused. "I acted the same way when I was her age. Boys didn't interest me."

She hesitated before asking a question that had been niggling her mind. "Why do you think Briann chose Cammy to come with her on the cruise?"

"That's my fault," said Jack as he picked up the pace again. "I assumed she'd have a miserable time if she came without a friend. Looking back on it, Briann would have had more fun rooming with my mom."

They walked another lap around the ship before Heather said, "Let's put on our bathing suits and give your mom a break from the girls. She's not the sun goddess she once was."

Jack gave his head a firm nod. "She'll be in the shade, covered from head to toe with yards of fabric and zinc-oxide painted on her nose and cheeks."

Heather asked, "What time is it?"

"It's hard to tell on cruise ships, but by the location of the sun, I'd say it's around two-thirty."

They made the trip upstairs to their rooms into something of a race. Heather took a cold shower after taking off only her shoes. She hung the quasi-clean clothes on a retractable line inside her shower, dried herself, and slipped into her bathing suit. She donned a knee-length sheer cover-up and a wide-brimmed hat. Jack waited for her in the hallway.

Once on the Lido deck, she looked for three familiar faces but found only two. Briann lay on a chaise lounge in the shade with her head elevated, reading a book. Jack's mother was next to her with her book folded across her chest. Otherwise, she was exactly how Jack said his mother would appear, taking every precaution against the scorching sun, even though she was in the shade.

Jack looked down at his daughter. "Where's Cammy?"

Briann looked up through sunglasses with huge, dark lenses. Her voice held more than a hint of frustration. "There's another pool on the rear deck. You should find her there."

"I thought you two were going to stay together."

"She didn't like the vibe of this pool."

Heather said, "I'll look for her."

Briann went back to her book but gave a parting comment. "You can't miss her. She'll be the center of attention."

Heather dreaded finding Cammy in the middle of a covey of older boys. She took her time walking among the sun worshippers then let out a gasp when she saw the teen. Cammy slept on her stomach, her skimpy bikini barely covering her intimate areas, let alone her back and legs. Heather touched a shoulder that felt like it came out of a pizza oven. "Wake up, Cammy."

"Huh?"

"Wake up. You've cooked yourself."

Her words slurred out. "I must have dozed off."

It was then that Heather noticed a stack of empty plastic glasses. She picked them up and smelled the pungent aroma of fruity rum.

"It must have been quite a party. Let's get you up to your room."

The wobbly teen turned over and let out a screech.

"You'd better hope someone brought an enormous bottle of

101

aloe vera. Your back is firetruck-red, but it's nothing like those two scarlet cheeks you failed to cover."

Heather helped her to her feet. "Where's your cover-up?"

"I don't know." She took three steps and stopped. "Wait. I remember. Briann took it when she left me. We had an argument when she saw my new bathing suit."

"That's not a bathing suit, it's a bandanna cut into three pieces held together with strings."

Panic widened Cammy's eyes. "If my mother finds out, she'll kill me."

It wasn't the time or place to pass out sage advice, so Heather walked on while supporting the girl.

# Chapter Thirteen

Jack's mother gasped when she saw Heather assisting Cammy into the shady portion of the Lido deck. Jack had his back to the approaching duo but jerked his head around and shot to his feet. Briann was already coming toward them with her friend's cover-up in her hand. She circled Cammy, draped the flimsy garment over her shoulders, and shouted, "You goober brain. I told you to be careful."

As Heather expected, tears flowed from the mostly-naked teen in a woman's body.

"Quit crying," said Briann with authority. "Your cheeks are the color of ripe strawberries and your back and legs aren't much better. Did you forget to put sunscreen on your backside?"

"Uh-huh," said Cammy through alcohol fumes.

"Did that guy buy you drinks?"

"Sort of. I gave him cash."

Cora arrived and took over. "Let's get her to your room. Briann, you take one side and I'll take the other."

"And button your top," scolded Briann. "If you wanted attention, you succeeded. Everyone's staring at you."

Cammy pleaded with Briann, "Stop hollering at me. I can barely walk."

"If you think walking is bad, wait until you try to sit."

"I want to go home."

Heather and Jack followed behind until they passed Heather's room. "I didn't pack, but maybe Pam thought to include aloe vera. I'll check."

"Take your time. I'm sure Mom will put her in the shower to sober her up and cool her off."

"That sounds like words of experience."

"I celebrated one too many times in high school. I made it to the front porch and thought it would be a good place to sleep. It wasn't a tepid shower but cold water from a garden hose that woke me. Dad had me up a ladder at dawn cleaning out the gutters. He worked me until dark."

"Did that break you from drinking?"

"It broke me from two things: drinking to excess and sleeping on the porch."

"You received a great lesson in tough love."

"I sure haven't forgotten it."

"Run on and check on Briann. She needs you."

Heather delivered the gooey remedy for minor burns to Cora then joined Jack in his connecting room.

Cora opened the connecting door and joined the two of them. "She's clean, slathered down, and laying sunny side up with only a sheet between her and the ceiling. I expect her to kick it off before long. Briann's watching television, and all Cammy can say is how much she wants to go home."

"Mom," said Jack in a firm voice, "we've taken advantage of you too much on this trip. I didn't intend for you to be a chaperon to a girl trying to grow up too fast."

His mother's lack of response told Heather this wasn't the trip she'd envisioned either.

Briann picked that moment to join them, closing the door behind her.

Jack kept talking. "I suggest we have an adult-only night." He shifted his gaze to Heather. "Do you agree?"

Before she could respond, Briann spoke. "I'm the one who asked Cammy to come along. That makes me responsible for her."

Jack gave a nod of approval. "When you get hungry, call room service and order whatever you want."

"Thanks, Dad. It will be pizza, salad, and soft drinks. I may splurge and get some cookies."

Cora gave Briann another instruction. "You may need to reapply the aloe several times. Keep the skin moist."

"I will, Grandma."

Heather picked up the ship's phone in Jack's room and dialed a number. A woman answered, "Ship's spa, how can we serve you?"

"What treatments do you have open?"

"Can you come right away?"

"Yes."

"How long would you like the treatment to last?"

"About an hour, perhaps two."

"You're in luck. We have several options to choose from. There are one-hour herbal poultice massages, or Swedish massages. There's also our hydro-pool therapy, steam and dry saunas, as well as our cold room. Only one manicurist or stylist is available right now."

"This is Heather McBlythe. Two women and a very handsome man are on our way. We'll decide what to get after we arrive." She hung up the phone. "Adult time begins now."

"Bummer," said Briann. "I've never had a real massage, only what my mom used to give me."

Heather looked at Jack who shrugged. She turned to Briann. "We'll see how Cammy is feeling tomorrow. Tonight, you stay with her."

---

HEATHER NOTED her father's confident stride as he walked side by side with Cora down the long hallway leading to the ship's main dining room. His full complement of silver hair seemed to shimmer whenever he passed under a recessed light in the ceiling. The tailored, dark navy suit fit his long, lean frame to perfection.

Upon arrival, he approached the maître d'. "McBlythe. Reservations for four."

The man's expression changed from harried to that of someone with only a single task to perform. "We've been expecting you, Mr. McBlythe." He motioned with a simple crook of his index finger for a waiting server to come forward. "Take Mr. McBlythe and his party to table twenty-seven."

The man gave the slightest of bows. "Please follow me."

They walked to a table at the back of the dining room beside a massive window overlooking the ship's wake and a spectacular view of the setting sun. Unlike the other servers, the man who guided them to their table had strands of silver below a bald dome. He motioned for Cora to be seated by extending a hand and pulling out her chair. Jack did the same for Heather. Her former fiancé and current boyfriend loved to hunt and fish, but he could morph to fit almost any occasion.

The tuxedo-wearing server made a general announcement with a heavy French accent. "*Bonsoir*. My name is Jean-Claude. I'll be serving you tonight and it is my goal to make this an *expérience exceptionelle*. As you can see, the sommelier has selected a bottle of the ship's finest champagne to start the evening's meal. Shall I pour, or would anyone like a cocktail instead?"

"I'd like the wine," said Heather.

"Me, too," said Cora.

Allister went next. "Scotch and soda, don't drown the Scotch."

"Bourbon on the rocks," said Jack.

"I'll return with the gentlemen's drinks and serve the wine."

The server seemed to glide, rather than walk, through the maze of tables.

Heather cast her gaze at her father. "Dad, did you have a pleasant day?"

Allister's words sounded pinched. "Mixed. I've had better. I had a long meeting with one of the vice presidents of the cruise line and the ship's captain. Their projections for growth and continued profits match what my people came up with."

"That was the good news. What's the bad? A fox among the chickens?" asked Heather.

"I wish it was only one fox. It seems there's an infestation of secret-sellers back in Boston. It must be the trendy thing to do. I've identified three so far; I fired one before I left."

"Now you believe there are two others?"

He spoke through clenched teeth. "It appears so."

"Are you sure?"

"Not yet."

Heather let the subject drop and turned her gaze to Cora, who was looking at the sun dip below the water.

Allister looked at Cora and spoke in a repentant voice. "I'm sorry. You didn't come along to talk business. Please forgive me. A pleasure cruise isn't the place to give voice to my petty woes. Tonight's dinner and show promises to lighten the mood."

"No need to apologize," said Cora. "I find the intrigue of big business fascinating."

Jean-Claude returned with the men's drinks. He then made a display of removing the bottle of wine from a silver wine bucket on a stand, wrapped it in a white towel, and uncorked it. He gave the cork to Allister, who sniffed it and nodded his approval. After observing the rest of the rituals, Jean-Claude served the ladies and left the table again.

Cora made a confession. "This type of service is new to me."

Jack patted his mother's hand. "Relax, Mom. You're among friends."

Heather hadn't considered how uncomfortable Cora felt with what her father considered normal. She looked around the room. Most of the men wore button-down shirts with off-the-rack pants while the women wore what she would consider office casual. Gone were the days of tuxedos for men and gowns for women. She'd committed her own faux pas by not telling Cora to bring an upscale dress. Then she remembered she didn't have a chance to pack for herself, much less advise Jack's mom on what to bring.

Jean-Claude delivered menus and retreated to a spot on the carpet that was near enough to attend to their every need, but far enough away to make it appear he wasn't interested in their conversation.

Jack took his turn at starting a conversation. "Allister, we had our own crisis to deal with today."

"Oh?"

"The young lady my daughter invited to come along on the cruise is dealing with a sunburn she'll not soon forget."

Heather lowered her voice and whispered, "She's in a

terrible hurry to grow up and made some choices that she's regretting."

"What choices?" asked Allister.

Heather answered. "Do you remember the time I raided the chalet's liquor cabinet on my fourteenth birthday?"

"How could I forget? I didn't believe it was possible that someone could heave for that long without doing permanent damage. Why you chose peppermint schnapps is beyond me."

"It seemed like the thing to do. I was trying to impress a cute Swiss boy, and it was cold unless I stood by the fire. The schnapps warmed me from the inside out."

Jack broke into the conversation. "Cammy's drinking led to something much worse than a hangover. She fell asleep in the afternoon sun."

Heather quickly added, "I'll not go into details, but Cammy also made a poor choice in swimwear. It was rather revealing."

Jack resorted to hyperbole. "I've seen more cotton in the top of an aspirin bottle."

Cora shook her head. "Poor thing. She'll stay in her room for the rest of the voyage and miss all the excursions we planned." She took a sip of champagne and replaced her glass. "I can't say that I would be too disappointed about that. Riding a zip line through a tropical forest, swimming with stingrays, and climbing ruins with my gimpy knee aren't really at the top of my list of things to do."

Jack let out a sigh. "I called Cammy's parents this afternoon. They couldn't apologize enough. I had a hard time talking them out of purchasing a ticket for a flight home from the Cayman Islands."

Jack buttered a roll then made quick work of eating it. Heather studied the faces of the other three. She looked at her father. "Who are we kidding? This trip is turning into the equivalent of a jail sentence, but with better food and softer beds. Dad, you need to get back to Boston and sort out what's going on at your office. Jack, you'd have more fun playing golf or fishing at the lake."

"Only if you and my bass boat were with me."

She looked at Cora. "Admit it. You're not having fun, either."

"I'm fine. The ship is lovely, and I loved sitting on the balcony early this morning."

The hesitation in her voice didn't fool Jack. "That was before the girls woke up and you felt responsible for them."

"That's not completely true. If it was me and Briann, we'd have a marvelous time."

Allister took his turn. "Heather, you've said nothing about your desire to be back in Texas. Steve's working a case and you're not there to help him."

Heather didn't deny it, and a cloud of silence fell over the table.

Allister took the napkin off his lap and placed it on his plate. He signaled for Jean-Claude to come to him.

"Are you ready for appetizers? Another drink?"

"We've had a change of plans." He looked at Heather. "I need to call my pilots. How does pizza and salads in my room sound?"

"Like heaven," said Heather. "We'll change, eat more pizza than we should, and go to the Lido deck. We'll sit under the stars on loungers and watch a movie."

Jack held up a hand to slow things down. "I'll come if I can have a cold beer."

"Me, too," said Cora.

Allister turned to Jean-Claude, who looked like he'd swallowed a bad oyster. "Send two deluxe pizzas to my room and four salads."

"Of course. I trust I did nothing to make this an unpleasant experience for you."

"On the contrary. The captain will receive a glowing report concerning your service."

Heather walked arm in arm with Cora through the dining room. Once they entered the hall, Cora leaned into her and whispered. "What's happening?"

"Father's jet will pick us up tomorrow morning at the airport near Montego Bay. We're going home."

# Chapter Fourteen

Heather and Jack's meeting with Cammy's parents took more time than she wanted it to. Jack had been stingy in revealing details of their daughter's misdeeds over the phone, and they wanted a full account. Fortunately, the sun-scorched teen made a complete *mea culpa* when prompted by her mother. All Jack had to do was get the words started with an opening statement. Cammy took over, and to her credit, confessed all. Then, she confessed it again, along with some other sins.

Mercy wasn't in her mother's eyes or voice, but Cammy's father took a gentler, but firm, attitude toward his daughter's misdeeds. He tried to hug her, but his arm draped across her shoulders was one more thing she wanted but couldn't have. Tears of teenage remorse and physical pain flowed freely.

Heather turned from the family scene and delivered hugs to the remaining passengers who had flown with them from Montego Bay, Jamaica to Conroe's regional airport.

Jack finished with Cammy's family and rejoined Heather,

who said, "We'll both be busy for the foreseeable future. Let's plan on doing something after Steve and I solve another one."

"I'll take you up on that rain check of a vacation with you."

"What about something like a barefoot sailing ship? It's been forever since I sailed. I hear they let you fish off those, or at least spearfish for your supper. I'm sure neither of us will forget our sunblock."

"I sure won't. I'll even trade in my Speedo for an extra baggy bathing suit."

Heather shuddered. "My bum stings just thinking about wearing something that exposes skin that never sees the sun."

Jack took her hand in his. "Don't forget that you'll be moving soon. We'll need to schedule our time away around that."

Heather dropped his hand and looked at him with wide eyes. "Did the sun cook my brain? I completely forgot we'll soon move."

Rasheed appeared with Princess, who pranced for joy at the sight of her mother. Heather rewarded her furry child with fingertips running through the dog's fur from ears to rump and back again. "Hello, my sweet girl. Did you and Le Roi behave yourselves?"

She continued to love on the dog while her father and Rasheed greeted each other. Her father led things off. "Did Steve have anything to say about the background information we sent him?"

"He did, indeed, and is most grateful. He wasn't expecting reports on every member of the Clay family."

"It was a group effort. Heather gave each of us an assignment then compiled all the information we gathered."

"With enough hands working, there are few blisters," said Rasheed.

Heather looked up from her kneeling position. "You made that up, didn't you?"

"I am compiling a book of original proverbs. So far, I have seventeen."

"How long have you been writing them?"

"Six years. My muse is very unreliable."

Allister's pilot closed the distance from the door leading to the tarmac to where Heather's father stood. "We're finished refueling, Mr. McBlythe."

Her father acknowledged the message with a nod. "I'll lose an hour in flight, so I'd better be off. Good luck with your investigation. Remember, you and Steve are to meet with Stewart Clay tomorrow morning at ten-thirty."

"Thanks, Daddy. Steve's elated you scored the meeting for us."

"You'll be in your new home the next time I see you."

"And your room will have a view of the lake."

She gave him a firm hug, which he returned and whispered, "I'm so proud of you, my precious daughter. So proud."

Heather felt her chin quiver as she watched her father stride toward the door. She felt Princess rub against her leg. A glance down revealed the dog holding the end of her leash in her mouth.

"Let's find Steve and Le Roi. There's a murder to solve and we won't do it standing here."

---

STEVE LIFTED his head before Le Roi barked. "I beat you this time," he said to his dog. He stuffed his phone back into his pocket and said, "Heather's home."

They walked out the door leading to the garage as the door lifted. He and Le Roi stepped in front of the car.

Rasheed opened his door. "Are we leaving?"

"Put Le Roi in the back."

"It's full of suitcases. Princess is in the back seat."

"Throw the suitcases out."

Heather bolted out her door. "What's wrong?"

"Get in. I'll explain on the way."

The sound of suitcases and travel bags sliding on the garage floor reached Steve's ears. Doors slammed.

"What's our destination?" asked Rasheed.

"The animal hospital," said Steve.

Heather's words came out laced with panic. "Where's Max?"

"He's where we're going."

Tires squealed as the car shot backward.

"Buckle up," said Steve. "Bella and I had just arrived home. She noticed Max lying in the backyard, next to the fence. She found a bowl with green liquid in it."

"Antifreeze," said Heather.

"Probably. Bella scooped Max up and ran to her car. I'm surprised you didn't pass her on your way in. I had just gotten off the phone with the animal hospital when I heard your car."

"Was Max still breathing?" asked Heather.

"He was when they left."

"Did you call the police?"

"Not yet. We left everything as is."

"Did Bella see anything?"

"No. It's more likely someone came this morning after Le Roi and I left for the office. He would have let me know if anyone had been here during the night. That narrows it down to between seven-thirty this morning and about the time you landed. Bella brought me home when Rasheed went to the airport to get you."

Steve waited for Heather to say something, but not a sound

came from her. He then said, "Rasheed and I will come in with you, but we can't stay long. He'll take me home so the police can get into the backyard."

Steve didn't know how she'd react if Max didn't make it, so he gave her something to do. "Call Jack. You don't need to be alone."

Heather did so and remained calm as she related the story. He counted this as a major victory. Six months ago, she wouldn't have coped well with the news that someone had tried to kill her beloved cat. So far, she'd remained calm and clear-headed. The genuine test would come if Max didn't pull through.

"Steve," said Heather after she completed the call with Jack. "After we solve the case in Houston, I want us to go after Bucky."

"It's a deal, partner."

Rasheed spoke as he brought the car to a sliding stop at the emergency entrance to the pet hospital. "Go, Heather. I'll bring Steve."

Heather had her door open before Rasheed finished his sentence. Bella met her three steps inside the door.

"Is Max..."

Bella cut in as words stuck in Heather's throat. "They took him from me the second I arrived. The vet listened to his heart-beat and said, 'No time to waste.' He gave a bunch of orders, but they meant nothing to me. A young woman wearing scrubs told me to wait here and someone would give me a report as soon as they could."

Heather closed her eyes for several seconds before opening them again. Steve, Rasheed, and both dogs came through the door. Heather answered their unasked question. "No word yet."

Bella sounded encouraging. "He had a heartbeat when we arrived."

Steve took his hand from the lead attached to Le Roi's vest and extended it for Heather to take. She gripped it and he squeezed. The wordless gesture somehow transferred a measure of peace and strength.

The touch didn't last long, but the feeling of not being alone remained.

Rasheed spoke in a soft tone. "Steve, we must leave."

He nodded. "Jack will be here soon. The police are on their way to the house. We'll be back as soon as the police finish collecting evidence."

"There won't be any," said Heather.

"We might get lucky this time."

Rasheed handed Heather Princess's leather leash.

Bella said, "Let's sit down. We may be here a long time."

"I hope so," said Steve. "This is one time when no news is most likely good news."

Heather sat beside Bella while Princess rested her head on Heather's lap. The feel of fur under her hand and the steady rhythm of the shepherd's breathing brought back memories of the many years Max had snuggled next to her. He'd seen her through many things, the good and the bad.

A clock on the wall grudgingly ticked off seconds then minutes. At least that's what Heather perceived. The logical part of her brain argued that time passed at the same rate, regardless of circumstances. She told logic to shove off and leave her alone. Her gaze alternated between the door leading to the treatment rooms and the one with a view of the parking lot. It was the latter that opened first, and Jack stepped through it.

Long strides brought him to her. She didn't remember standing, but the sensation of his arms around her brought comfort then tears. He had always shown patience with her, and this crisis was no different. A second set of arms wrapped around her back. She hadn't noticed her arrival, but Briann held her, too.

Bella dispensed the limited information. "We're still waiting to hear."

Heather turned to face Briann, who looked at her with red-rimmed eyes. "Dad said Max may not make it."

"What does he know?" said Heather with false bravado as she brushed a lock of hair from the teen's face. "He's just a lawyer, not a veterinarian. My money's on Max."

"Mine, too," said Bella.

The words seemed to lift some of Briann's fears, but not all. She'd watched her mother succumb to the effects of cancer. Death was more real to her than most young ladies her age.

Heather wanted to get the teen's thoughts to a better place, so she sat down and motioned for Jack to sit on her right and Briann on her left. She then spoke to Princess. "Give Briann love."

The shepherd shifted her attention to the teen and received repeated strokes on her head.

*So far, so good*, thought Heather to herself. "Have you heard from Cammy?"

"Her mom took her phone at the airport. There's no telling when she'll get it back." She took a deep breath. "I heard from Julie Shropshire. She said pictures of Cammy are all over the internet. The guy on the ship who bought drinks for her posted them. They show her face in some, but most are of her sunburned backside."

Jack chimed in. "Let that be a lesson to you."

Briann pursed her lips. "I feel like I didn't do enough to protect her."

"I feel the same way about Max," said Heather.

More minutes passed in silence before the door leading to the treatment rooms opened. The vet walked toward them. She reached instinctively for Jack's and Briann's hands.

"Hello, Heather," said the middle-aged man. "It's too soon to know for sure, but I'm optimistic that Max is going to make it. We induced vomiting and flushed his stomach with activated charcoal and sodium sulfate. After that, I gave him a dose of ethanol."

Jack questioned the treatment. "You gave Max a shot of booze?"

The vet nodded. "Ethyl alcohol and a medicine called fomepizole can save a cat if administered in time. I gave Max a measured dose of ethanol and started him on an IV. The ethylene glycol in antifreeze attacks the kidneys. Cats are twice as susceptible to antifreeze as dogs of a similar size." He took a breath and continued, "And speaking of size, I believe that's what saved Max. He's extra-large, even for a Maine coon."

"What's the bad news?" asked Heather.

"Not as much as I thought there would be when he came in. It's his kidneys that give me the most concern. We'll keep him on IVs for two or three days. The more he pees, the better the chances he won't need dialysis."

Heather asked, "Can we see him?"

"Sure. Come on back."

As Heather stroked his head, Max rallied and ran a rough tongue across the back of her hand. When he laid his head down again and closed his eyes, Heather, Jack and Briann returned to the waiting room to give Bella the good report.

Taking her dog's lead from Bella, Heather said, "There's really nothing else we can do for Max. You should go home to Adam." Holding the lead with one hand, she wrapped the other arm around Bella's shoulders and said, "Thank you for taking care of him."

"I'm so glad I got him here in time. He'll be curled up on your bed again before you know it."

Heather gave her a weak smile of acknowledgment. Bella said good-bye to them and headed toward her SUV.

Jack looked at Heather and asked, "Are you sure you're okay leaving now?"

Heather nodded. "I'm sure. He's in good hands and they'll call if anything changes. I'll go let the receptionist know we're leaving."

Once in Jack's truck, he asked, "Do you have anything to eat at your house?"

"Not much."

"Me, either. I was planning on gaining weight on the ship all week."

"I'll call Steve, give him the good news, and see what he and Rasheed want."

Steve took the good news in stride. "We wasted a lot of time and words worrying about Max's weight. Being tubby saved his life. Stop by the Burger Barn and get me the usual and add a chocolate milkshake."

"You'll have to spend an extra thirty minutes on the treadmill tomorrow morning."

"I'll chance it. Will you be all right going to Houston with me tomorrow?"

"More than all right. Max will be safe, and I'll go crazy if I'm standing still."

"By the way," said Steve. "Moving day got moved up again. Crews will be here early tomorrow. We'll spend tomorrow night in our new homes."

# Chapter Fifteen

Heather rose before dawn, too excited to sleep any longer. Her thoughts reminded her of the clicking wheel of a carnival game, landing on something different with almost every spin. The first was Max, wondering how he'd spent the night. The next was the long-awaited day of moving to her dream home on the lake. She couldn't have asked for a better housemate than Steve, but they each wanted their own home. When God made the two of them, he used an extra wide brush to paint in an independent streak. Close, but not too close, was the life they both desired.

The imaginary wheel spun again and settled on the murder of Dan Clay. It seemed like forever since her inner circle of friends had traveled to the San Jacinto Monument. Steve, with help from his gift of associative chromesthesia, announced that the son of a prominent oil baron didn't commit suicide. The last spin of the wheel settled on Cindy Clay, the sister of the murdered politician. What hold did Claire Strobel, the environmental activist, have over her? Was Cindy estranged from all her family members? Could she have been manipulated to harm her brother?

She and Steve had a lot to talk about on the way to Houston. But first, it was time to put on leggings and break out her yoga mat. Earbuds played the soothing voice of an instructor who gave directions to assume positions and how long to hold them. Muscles and ligaments stretched. Princess watched, her head occasionally tilting when Heather struck a difficult pose.

The yoga mat returned to its spot in the closet and Heather made her bed for the last time in this house. Then she realized her mistake, tore off the bed linens, and stuffed everything into large, black, plastic bags.

She heard Steve rummaging in the kitchen and joined him. They kept the banter light, both content to spend long periods in silence. A few strawberries, blueberries, and the unbruised half of the last banana sufficed for breakfast.

Following a quick shower, she dried her hair, pulled it back with a scrunchie, and applied a light amount of makeup. As she applied her mascara, she wondered again why she couldn't do so without her mouth opening. She looked like a fish out of water. Do all women do that? Heather shook her head to clear it of such random thoughts. She had plenty of rational questions to ponder.

Pam, her personal assistant, arrived with a platoon of packers and movers. The reality that their home would be empty before noon hit her.

Rasheed arrived next, and Steve came from his apartment with Le Roi leading the way, looking dignified.

Steve must have smelled her perfume. "We'd better leave before Pam stuffs us in boxes and we miss our appointment."

Rasheed spoke next. "I parked on the street some distance away. It's a perfect day to move, overcast and a light breeze."

Heather said, "We still have time to stop and see Max."

"Perfect," said Steve. "I don't want him to think we abandoned him."

Steve called it the collar of shame when he felt the plastic ring around Max's neck. "Don't worry, old friend, you'll get it off soon enough and you'll have a beach to explore when you get out of kitty jail."

Heather scratched Max's rump, and he responded by arching his back. "You look so much better than you did last night."

He purred and flexed his claws.

"Time to go," said Steve.

They returned to the car where Rasheed waited with the motor running and the air conditioner on. The temperature was already pushing ninety but not expected to rise much more.

Steve took his usual position in the back seat. The acoustics of the car were so good he had no trouble hearing Heather, even as she faced forward. The car had barely cleared the parking lot when he said, "Let's review what we know about the victim. You go first, Heather."

She wondered if this was a test to make sure her mind could focus properly on the case. She searched her memory. "Dan Clay. Married once to Angelica Rojas-Clay-Flores. Native of Argentina. Their college romance lasted six years until they divorced, and she returned to Argentina. She remarried and now resides in Buenos Aires with her second oil-executive husband and four children. The fifth is on the way. Reason for divorce from Dan Clay is his lack of desire for children."

"Any possibility she's involved in his murder?"

"Slim to none, leaning heavily to none."

"Did Dan have any serious relationships after Angelica?"

"Plenty of relationships, but none I would describe as serious. He liked to be seen with high-style women of the fashion model persuasion. Long legs, thick lips, and stares of indifference marked the ones who caught his eye."

Steve took in the information without further comment about the women who came in and out of the victim's life. "Let's go over the crime scene at the monument. Does anything stand out to you?"

"Yeah. It seemed staged."

Rasheed gave her a look that asked her to explain. Steve used his words for the same purpose.

"First," said Heather, "It was too clean. No prints inside or outside of his car on the driver's side."

"What does that tell you?"

Heather let out a huff of exasperation. "Is this a game show where I get points for correct answers?"

"Sorry," said Steve. "I like to ask questions I've already answered. It's an old habit that helps me think."

Heather murmured, "My old habit is to get offended over small things, like a partner questioning me."

Steve responded with a soft chuckle. "We're both out of practice. Let's start over."

"At the beginning?"

"No. The crime scene. What else did you observe at the crime scene or in the reports other than a too-clean car?"

"The police reports said they found a mostly empty bottle of Scotch by the reflecting pool. It reminded me of a stage prop."

"Scotch is what the coroner found in Dan's stomach. Doesn't that give credence to the theory that he killed himself?"

"That's the problem," said Heather. "I know beyond all doubt that Dan didn't kill himself."

Rasheed interrupted. "Ms. Heather, how can you be so sure?"

Heather realized she'd said too much. Rasheed didn't know about Steve's ability to see red, and Steve wanted it to remain that way. He came to her rescue by saying, "It's magic, Rasheed. I have a crystal ball I look into to see the past."

"You jerk my foot again, my friend."

"Are you sure I'm not pulling your leg?"

"You say half a dozen, I say thirty-four minus twenty-eight."

Steve gave him a pat on the shoulder. "Houston traffic lends itself to accidents. You drive and save the questions for later. After all, the mouth that speaks when driving in Houston is married to the hand that signs a ticket for causing an accident."

"That proverb will go on the rejection list for my book."

Steve then asked, "Where were we?"

"The bottle of booze," said Heather.

"Scotch," said Steve. "Do we know what brand?"

"If I remember, it was Johnny Walker."

"Uh-huh. Black Label. What else do we know about the crime scene?"

"The cause of death was drowning. The abrasion on Dan's head was superficial, more of a scrape than a blow."

"Do you think someone held him underwater?"

Heather took her time before responding, "I do. At least one person and possibly two or three."

Steve shifted in the back seat. "The coroner found no fibers or skin under Dan's fingernails. What does that tell us?"

"I know," said Rasheed. "The victim didn't struggle. I read it last night in a Nero Wolfe mystery book."

Steve challenged him. "That's only one possibility, and keep your eyes on the road. Your voice increased when you turned your head."

"Rasheed is right that Dan didn't struggle," said Heather.

"The only reason I can give is perhaps he was too drunk and drugged." She then said, "It's your turn, Steve. What are other reasons for him not fighting to live?"

"I don't know him well enough yet. What interests me more is the location. Why the reflecting pool at the scene of such a historic battle? Think about it. A minimum of two people were involved. We know this because someone had to drive his car and leave it in the parking lot on the ship channel side of Independence Parkway."

"Are you sure?" asked Heather.

Steve answered her with a question of his own. "It's summer. If he had been in his car in the parking lot, forensics would have found his fingerprints there. No gloves were in his car, and he wasn't wearing any in the water."

"But the report said they found his fingerprints in the car," said Heather.

"Not on the steering wheel or the driver's door. Someone else wiped those areas clean."

Heather grumbled under her breath. "You win this one."

Steve pressed on. "We know he was heavily under the influence of alcohol, and we've determined he didn't drive himself to the reflecting pool. It's past midnight and before dawn. Of all places to take him to kill him, why the reflecting pool?"

He slowed the pace of his next question. "Perhaps it has something to do with history. Someone went to a lot of trouble to take Dan Clay to an almost two-hundred-year-old battlefield to kill him. Why?"

Heather puffed out her cheeks and blew out a breath. "Do you really think this has something to do with history?"

"Either it does, or someone wants us to think it does." He added a postscript. "Of course, I could be wrong."

Steve's agile mind took a sharp turn, which sometimes

happened when working a case. The squeak of leather sounded, meaning he'd leaned back in his seat. "Heather, I want you and Bella to take another pass at our victim's sister, Cindy. We need to confirm her estrangement from her father and brother."

"I'll have to arrange something to separate her from Claire Strobel."

"Do what you have to, but I'd like it done by tomorrow night."

Heather whispered, "Nothing like an impossible deadline."

"Nonsense," said Steve. "Your head and emotions are running like a Swiss clock. You and Bella should be able to come up with a plan this afternoon while she's helping you unpack boxes. Implement it tomorrow and write the report. Piece of cake."

She responded under her breath. "More like a mud pie."

"What's that?" asked Steve.

Heather issued an intentional lie. "I asked if you wanted ice cream on your pie when we celebrate moving into our new homes tonight."

"I didn't know we were having a move-in celebration. That sounds like fun. Is Jack making the arrangements?"

"I'll call Pam. Jack's lousy at planning parties."

"How about I call your PA? You can call the vet. Make sure Max is still doing okay. I'm having a hard time thinking about anything but my nap buddy."

Rasheed spoke next. "We're four minutes from our destination. I suggest haste in making your phone calls."

# Chapter Sixteen

R asheed wheeled Heather's car onto the driveway of a
home in the prestigious River Oaks area of Houston. A
tall metal gate blocked them from entering until Rasheed used
the intercom/camera combination mounted on a pole to identify himself, Heather, and Steve. The metal gate swung open,
and they advanced.

"How tight is the security?" asked Steve.

"What I expected," said Heather. "High walls, cameras
hidden in fake birdhouses, a couple of guards dressed to look
like gardeners. It's enough to deter without giving the place the
look of an armed camp. To the untrained eye, it looks like any
of fifty other homes in this part of Houston."

She added, "If I could get a look at their surveillance room,
I could tell you a lot more."

"No need," said Steve. "From what you said about the
gardeners, Stewart Clay is prepared for uninvited visitors. Any
sign of dogs?"

"None that I see, but you can bet they're roaming the
grounds at night."

Steve said, "Rasheed, you stay in the car with Princess. Heather, Le Roi and I will go in. There's no point pressing our luck with two dogs."

"Can I let her out for a few minutes?"

"Good idea," said Heather. "Let her sniff around. You'll be able to tell if she alerts to the presence of other dogs. She'll want to track, but don't allow it."

"I'll keep a firm grip on her leash."

The front door opened and a broad-shouldered man wearing a coat and tie came out and stood at the top of the brick steps. He wasn't smiling.

Rasheed went to the back of the car and took Le Roi out. The giant schnauzer hurried to Steve's door and sat until he exited the car and took hold of the lead.

The man's countenance didn't change, but his posture became more rigid. "I wasn't told you were bringing a dog."

Steve spoke in a buoyant voice. "We actually brought two, but only one will stay with us. As you can see, he's trained to guide me."

"He's big for a guide dog."

"Big and lovable," said Steve. "One of his best friends is Ms. McBlythe's cat."

"Wait here until I put our dogs up. They're not what you would call docile around other dogs."

The man left and Heather sidled up to Steve. "That answers your question. Dogs inside during the day and outside at night."

It wasn't long before the man returned. He reminded Heather of a cross between a male model and a refrigerator. Close-cropped dark hair spoke of a military background, as did square shoulders on his suit jacket. "Please follow me. Mr. Clay is expecting both of you."

Heather went first, with Steve and Le Roi following close

behind. They crossed a marble-floored entryway with closed doors on the left and right. Judging from the windows that faced the front of the home, these doors likely led to a parlor, library, or perhaps, an office.

The entry expanded as they kept walking. An arching staircase wound itself upward to the second floor. The oak rail and balusters shone, daring any self-respecting dust mite to rest on them.

On they walked into the home's great room, and great it was in size. The decor mixed late nineteenth and twentieth century oil boom styles. Leather couches and chairs were artfully arranged for conversation. Lamps with miniature pump jacks on the base gave the room a soft glow. The artwork celebrated oil spewing skyward in various locations around the world. The only thing missing from the tribute to liquid gold was the smell of a refinery.

A man holding a stubby glass in his hand stood. The ice rattled in it as he set it on a table beside his chair. His first words took her aback. "Heather, you look more like your mother than your father."

"I take that as a compliment."

"You probably don't remember me, but I met you briefly when you were about this high." He lowered his hand to the height of his knees. "Your au pair came down with a cold while your mother was shopping, forcing your father to bring you to lunch. I'm not sure how much he paid the maître d' to find a server to feed and entertain you, but whatever it was, it was worth it. We both made a wad of money from the deal we made that day. He also had the good sense to sell before the wells played out."

She responded with a pinched smile. "That's my father, the man with the Midas touch."

Graying eyebrows lifted. "He says you have the same fairy whispering in your ear."

Heather shook her head. "My muse whispers; my father's shouts."

"Don't kid an old oil man. You're cut from the same cloth." His voice changed. "What's this about you being some sort of private investigator?" He threw up his hands. "Hold on. Where are my manners? Who's this with you?"

Steve jumped into the conversation. "Don't answer that, Heather. Mr. Clay knows who I am. He's already done his research and knows all about me."

"You're pretty sure of yourself, Mr. Smiley."

"I can prove it. I'll bet you five bucks you even know I specialize in recognizing deception, and I'll bet you another five you know my dog's name."

"I'll not take that bet. By gum, you're better than I thought. Your dog's name is Le Roi, The King, and Heather's dog is Princess. Do you mind if I check your dog over?"

Steve dropped the handle, took a step back, and gave Le Roi a command in French to not move.

Heather watched as the man gave Le Roi a tooth to tail inspection before stepping back. "I prefer Dobermans for security, but Le Roi outweighs mine by fifteen pounds. Is he really police and service trained?"

Steve nodded. "Dual certified with papers to prove it."

"You've impressed me with your dog, but what can you offer me that the police can't, in regard to putting my son's killer in prison?"

"Nothing until we sit down. You're ready for a fresh glass of Scotch and I'd like a beer. I'm sure Heather wouldn't turn down something since she's not driving."

"How did you know I wanted a fresh drink?"

"I heard the ice rattle in your glass. There's no liquid in it.

131

Also, you're grieving the loss of your son and drinking before noon. I know what it's like to lose someone."

Stewart nodded, even though Steve couldn't see him. "Before we go on, let's move to a room that's not such a cavern. I had no intention of paying much attention to anything either of you had to say, but now I've changed my mind."

"What changed your mind?" asked Heather, as they walked to a hidden door that looked like a paneled wall.

"A favor to your father got you in the house. Your accomplishments as a businesswoman got you into the great room. Your partner Steve and Le Roi made me want to hear what you have to say."

The room he led them into was a fraction of the size of the great room. It was like walking from a movie set about an oil baron to that of a moderately successful insurance salesman. Gone was any hint of sentimentality. The desk and chairs were built more for utility than comfort. Bookshelves and file drawers streamlined within the wall completed a room designed for utility and efficiency. The lone exception was a well-stocked bar, small refrigerator, and a countertop ice maker.

"What's your poison, Heather?" asked Stewart.

"White wine, if you have it."

"That's what I thought."

Stewart moved on to Steve. "A bottle or can of beer is all I can offer you. Nothing on tap."

"Bottle," said Steve.

Heather looked at the utilitarian desk while Stewart tinkered behind her and Steve. Their host delivered the drinks and took a seat on the boss's side of the desk.

Stewart drained half his glass before asking, "What can you tell me that the police haven't?"

Steve spoke with absolute confidence. "Your son's death

wasn't an accident. At least two people were involved in killing him."

"Finally," said Stewart in a firm voice. "Someone with common sense." A note of optimism came into his words. "Do you know who did it?"

"Not yet."

Stewart leaned forward. "I already know, but I can't prove it. Can you?"

Steve folded his collapsible cane and placed it on the floor. "You believe it's Bill Boyd working under Leonard Spears's direction."

"One hundred percent. Spears lost his inside track to information when my son beat him fair and square in the election."

"I'm not sure Spears sees it that way. You spent a lot of money winning that election. Then you made sure everyone knew it was Bill Boyd who killed Dan's campaign manager, and that Spears was behind the killing."

"And he spent even more getting Boyd out of prison."

"I heard, and I don't like it any more than you do. I was the cop who arrested Boyd and testified against him in court."

"I know you did, and you checked all the right boxes. It was some flunky attorney in the DA's office who screwed up. I'm telling you, Smiley, Bill Boyd killed my son. My only son."

"You might be right," said Steve. "Then again, there's a chance you're wrong."

Heather interrupted. "This is excellent wine. What brand is it?"

It was such a change of pace that it caused Stewart to sit slack jawed and silent.

Before he could gather his thoughts, Heather kept talking. "Tell us about your daughter, Cindy."

Stewart found his voice. "What does she have to do with anything?"

Heather continued, "Most likely nothing, but I'm not so sure about the company she keeps. I spoke with Cindy a few days ago while she was in the hospital in Galveston. I've never heard of anyone being beaten, cut with a knife, and shot without receiving serious wounds. They released her the next day. After meeting her friend Claire Strobel, I'm pretty sure she insisted on it."

"That woman is nothing but evil," snapped Stewart.

"I'll not argue with your assessment of Claire. She threw me and my friend out of Cindy's room." Heather leaned forward. "She also seems to have a strangle-hold on your daughter."

"My daughter's weak. Sweet and innocent, but she could use a hefty dose of common sense and a new backbone. Those crazy tree-huggers got their claws in her and won't let her go. It used to be animal rights until she put environmental causes on the top of her list of things to complain about."

Stewart sucked in a full breath through his nose then let it out. "I'll ask one more time, what does Cindy have to do with Dan's murder?"

Heather answered his question with an observation. "I witnessed how weak your daughter is when Claire Strobel entered the hospital room. Did Dan receive any threats you'd consider serious from anyone in the environmental movement?"

Stewart didn't need to consider the question. "Everyone in the oil business gets threats, including their family members."

Steve took over. "The police haven't even declared your son's death to be a murder. Suspicious, yes, but no determination of homicide."

"That's because the medical examiner is an incompetent twit."

"No, he's not," said Steve in an even voice. "He's arrogant

and prideful, but not incompetent. Your phone call to him was a mistake. So were the phone calls to half the politicians in the state. No wonder the police are moving so slowly. You burned bridges and got nothing from it but people slow-walking their jobs."

It was time for Heather to play good cop. "Let's all take a step back, finish our drinks, and take a fresh look at what we have and where we can go from here."

Steve tipped up his bottle and took a full swallow of his beer. Heather did the same with her wine. Stewart followed suit but drained his glass once again.

The break gave everyone time to get their emotions under control, even though Heather knew Steve had baited Stewart into losing his temper.

She got things going again by slowing her words and speaking softly. "What I'd like to point out is this: In three days, Steve and I have made significant progress. We've determined at least two people killed your son; we have the police reports, forensic reports, and the preliminary cause of death. We visited the crime scene and have identified multiple suspects."

Steve took over. "You're convinced Bill Boyd killed Dan. Like I said before, you may be right, but we've already provided you with another possibility—Claire Strobel or other radical environmentalists. There's another whole list of possibilities we haven't gotten to yet."

Stewart folded his hands together on his desk. "I know you're leading up to something. What is it?"

"We want you to take a step back and don't do anything you'll regret. You acted out of your emotions with politicians and law enforcement and got nowhere. You and Leonard Spears are preparing for war. We're coming into this murder without a preconceived idea of who killed Dan. Give us a chance to find the killers before there's more collateral damage than you bargained for. No one wins if the shooting starts."

Stewart countered with, "I retain the right to defend myself, my family, my property, and my businesses."

Steve lifted his chin. "Take whatever defensive steps you believe are necessary, prudent, and lawful. All Heather and I are asking for is a commitment from you that you'll give us time to discover who killed your son. When we identify them, we'll turn the case over to the appropriate authorities."

"How much time?"

Heather said, "As long as it takes."

"Not good enough. You wouldn't enter a contract that didn't have a start and end date."

Heather realized he was right; she'd made a foolish mistake.

Steve spoke up. "Two weeks, and we'll need full cooperation from you, your family members, and your head of security."

Stewart leaned back in his chair with hands clasped together, resting on his stomach. After several long seconds, he leaned forward again. "One week. I can't speak for my daughter, and my wife has a mind of her own. They may or may not cooperate. I'll give you my head of security to show I'm acting in good faith. He's former CIA."

Heather asked, "Is he the guy built like a tank who met us at the front door?"

He nodded. "Fred Lawrence is his name."

Steve asked, "Can I speak to him today?"

"Only if you agree to a one-week deadline."

Heather said, "I brought a standard contract with me. I'll fill in the special conditions and have it ready for your signature in about ten minutes."

"You two were pretty sure of yourself."

Heather responded with a weak smile. "My father told me you were a hard, but reasonable, man to do business with."

Steve said, "Heather signs all documents for me. I'd like to speak to Mr. Lawrence as soon as possible."

"What's the rush?"

"Heather and I are moving into our new homes at her lakeside development today. We'd like to focus on that as soon as possible."

Stewart shifted his gaze to her. "Your father told me how proud he is of you for pulling off that deal." He looked down at his hands. "I'm hoping my daughter comes around soon."

Heather said, "I'm planning to see her tomorrow—if I can separate her from Claire Strobel."

"Good luck with that," said Stewart.

Steve asked, "Do you keep tabs on Cindy?"

"Fred does."

Heather went to the minibar and placed her glass in the sink. "I'll knock out the contract and speak with Mr. Lawrence later."

Steve said, "While she's doing that, could I speak with your wife? And then maybe Mr. Lawrence."

"That's fine with me, but like I said, she has a mind of her own. She should be in her office. I'll get Fred to take you to her."

# Chapter Seventeen

S teve felt Heather take his half-empty bottle of beer from him as the door opened and he caught a whiff of Fred Lawrence's aftershave. Le Roi stood, as did Steve. He unfurled his cane then gripped the handle on his dog's lead and said, "Follow."

Once the door closed behind them, Steve said, "Your boss didn't use his phone to call, text, or notify you to come by pressing a button on or under the top of his desk. You watched and listened to the entire conversation."

"Are you sure he didn't buzz me?" asked the head of security.

"I'm sure. If he'd summoned you by using his phone, I'd have heard it. That door is thick, but not completely sound-proof. I'd have heard a buzzer go off on the other side."

"I could have been in another room."

"You came too fast to be in another room. No. You watched and listened to everything that went on in his office on your phone."

"I'm responsible for keeping Mr. Clay safe, and I take my job seriously."

Steve wanted to ask Fred if Stewart knew about the miniature cameras and microphones Fred had placed in his boss's office, but didn't. The man was a former spook. Keeping secrets was in his blood, even from his boss, if it meant enhancing his employer's safety.

Fred stopped before they walked out of the great room. "I underestimated you, Mr. Smiley. I'd appreciate it if Mr. Clay didn't know how serious I am about keeping him alive."

Steve said, "Since you saw and heard everything that took place in Mr. Clay's office, you already know our purpose in coming here. More importantly to you, we're not here to tattle on you for being overzealous in your duties. Besides, it's Stewart's fault for telling us you're ex-CIA. I wouldn't have thought of hidden cameras and microphones if he'd not blabbed that bit of information."

"Thank you for your discretion."

Steve stayed where he stood and asked, "What's the story that goes with his daughter, Cindy?"

The question seemed to slam into a wall of silence for at least several seconds. The wall developed a crack as Fred took in and let out a breath through his nose. "If you and Ms. McBlythe are as good as I'm told, nothing I'm about to say will come as a surprise. Cindy's the prodigal child. She's a plain girl who loves animals. When she went away to college, she studied environmental nonsense and got caught up in the whole save-the-planet movement."

"I understand her mother died when she was a small child."

"Cancer. That was before Mr. Clay lived in River Oaks, before I was employed by him. Once Cindy was in college, the activists brainwashed her into believing that living near the refineries caused her mom's lung cancer."

"What about Stewart? I noticed a rattle in his voice. He must be a smoker."

"A two-pack-a-day man until his first wife died. He still sneaks one when he's stressed."

"I caught a whiff in his office."

"Yeah. Dan's death has him dancing barefoot on broken lightbulbs. He thinks he's next to go."

Steve moved on. "Heather saw Cindy in the hospital several days ago. She's convinced Cindy's being exploited. What's your opinion?"

"Cindy's a trophy for the climate wackos. Claire Strobel marches her out from time to time to put a face with someone who saw the light and gave up a cushy life to worship trees. It tears Mr. Clay up every time he sees her on television."

"Do you know if Cindy is in your boss's will?"

"You'll have to ask his personal attorney. I protect him and he pays me well to do so."

"Perhaps you know this: Does he support Cindy financially?"

"She receives a modest allowance. It's only enough to put a roof over her head and food on the table. She lives in Galveston and gets around on an electric bicycle."

Steve took a step, and Le Roi matched him. "Thanks for talking to me."

"I wouldn't have if I thought you weren't trying to keep Mr. Clay alive."

Steve could tell by the sound of his footfalls that he was retracing the path he took on the way to the great room. "Right or left?" he asked as they approached the doors leading left and right.

Fred asked, "Did you count the steps or did the dog alert you?"

Steve kept a straight face. "That's a trade secret and I've trained the dog not to say a word."

It didn't last long, but Fred let out a muted chuckle. His voice reverted to his prior monotonous drone. "Mrs. Clay is expecting you."

Two knocks sounded on the door and a woman's voice said, "Come in."

The door opened, and Fred went in first. "Mrs. Clay, this is Steve Smiley and Le Roi, his guide dog."

Steve made out the sound of the woman rising from her chair and walking toward him. "Hello, Mr. Smiley. I'm Lisa Clay."

The two shook hands, which gave him an opportunity to smell her perfume. He couldn't place the name, but, thanks to Heather's tutelage, he knew the difference between a two-hundred and a two-thousand-dollar-an-ounce fragrance. This one fell into the second category.

"Not Roberts-Clay?" asked Steve.

"The hyphenated last name is something my publicist insists on. She thinks I need a separate identity to avoid confusion. After all, I'm the second Mrs. Clay."

"Ah," said Steve. "I can see the benefit of that."

"May I take you to a chair, Mr. Smiley?"

"Let me tell Le Roi not to tear your arm off. He's very protective of me."

"I'll take him," said Fred. "No need taking any chances."

Steve spoke in French to his dog, and in a matter of a few seconds, he sat with his dog lying on the carpet beside him.

He could tell by the other sounds that Lisa sat behind a desk in a leather chair as she began the conversation. "I'm at a loss to know why you want to talk to me, Mr. Smiley."

Fred answered before he could. "Mr. Smiley is a former homicide detective. His partner is Heather McBlythe. She's signing a contract with your husband to investigate Dan's murder."

"Oh? I didn't know the police had ruled it a murder."

"They haven't," said Steve. "Heather and I are going on the assumption that it is. We've been working on the case for several days and it has all the hallmarks of a well-planned and executed homicide."

"Finally, my husband has someone who's taking Dan's death seriously. He's been an emotional wreck ever since he received the phone call about Dan. It's been a nightmare living in fear that one of us could be next."

"From what I've heard from Fred and your husband, adequate precautions are in place to keep you safe. You couldn't ask for a more qualified chief of security, so we won't waste our time making recommendations related to protection. This will allow us to devote all our skills and energy to discovering who killed your stepson and why."

"But Stewart already knows. Didn't he tell you that Leonard Spears arranged for Bill Boyd's release from prison?"

Fred spoke up. "Mr. Smiley knows all about Spears and Boyd. He's the detective who arrested Boyd and testified against him."

"Really? Then you know how dangerous he is. It can't be a coincidence that Dan was killed within months of his release."

"I agree, and if your husband's suspicions are correct, the evidence should point directly to him. If that's the case, we'll gather it and turn it over to the police."

A long second passed before Lisa said, "Why do I have the impression that the next word from you will be, 'but?'"

"But," said Steve, "Heather and I must go where the evidence leads. I can name at least three other categories of people who might have killed Dan."

"Oh? Who?"

"First, environmentalists. Next, people who didn't like his politics. Third, people who feel your husband might have cheated them out of money. Big business has a way of creating big enemies. Also, never underestimate the money angle."

Fred spoke up. "That's why Mr. Clay believes Leonard Spears and Bill Boyd either did it or had it done for them. Spears had a cushy thing going when he served on the city council. Dan's victory put him out of the inner circle of knowing what's going to happen before it does."

Steve held his hands up with palms showing. "Don't get me wrong; I'm not debating against Spears and Boyd. All Heather and I want to do for the next six days is gather information. Mrs. Clay, I'd like to start with you."

"Me? I know nothing of the murder."

"You might be more helpful than you realize. Tell me about your stepdaughter."

"What do you want to know?"

"What was she like growing up?"

"Please don't tell me you believe she had anything to do with killing her brother."

"It's not beyond the realm of possibility. People can do amazing things if subjected to enough pressure."

"What do you think, Fred?" asked Lisa.

He took his time answering. "Steve's right. Professional brainwashing or hypnosis can get people to do almost anything. Repetition and constant stimuli can change a meek person into a remorseless killer."

"I guess you're right, but Cindy was always such a wall-flower. I can't imagine her taking someone's life."

Steve shrugged. "Perhaps she was the bait, not the killer. Would Dan have met her at a remote location like the San Jacinto monument late at night if she asked him to?"

"They weren't very close, but Dan had a soft spot for his kid sister."

Steve added, "There's nothing to show that Dan struggled with his assailants, but something got him to the battlefield to meet with people at such a late hour."

"You used the plural form of the noun," said Fred. "Do you believe there were multiple people who lured him to the battleground?"

"It would only take one to lure him, but we believe there were at least two involved."

Steve moved on. "I'd like to ask both of you to do something for us. I gave you possibilities of people who might have a motive for killing Dan. So far, we've focused on only two. That should keep Heather and me busy for two or three days. Could you work together to come up with the names of those who fall into other categories?"

"I have a list of radical environmentalists," said Fred.

"I'm not sure I can help much, but I also know a few people who have animus against Stewart for business deals," said Lisa.

Steve asked, "Was Dan as tough of a businessman as your husband?"

Fred answered, "Just as tough, smarter, and more... how shall I put this? More multi-dimensional."

"Slicker?" asked Steve.

"That's not an adjective I'd use, but I believe others might."

Steve stood, as did Le Roi. "Your husband is giving us only one week to find the persons responsible for Dan's death. I can't emphasize enough how important your help will be in bringing this investigation to a quick and successful conclusion."

Lisa stood. "We'll do all we can to help, starting this afternoon."

Steve thanked them, tilted his head, but didn't move. "Heather and Stewart are coming."

"I didn't hear anything," said Lisa.

"Le Roi and I did. It's a game we play, and the dog usually wins." He extended his hand to Lisa and felt a firm shake from a dainty hand.

A knock on the door sounded. Fred was already moving to open it. Heather came in first. "Pardon us for barging in. I'm Heather McBlythe. I told Stewart I wanted to meet you before Steve and I left."

"I feel like I already know you and Steve," said Lisa.

"Oh?"

"I read the book about Bella Brumley and saw the movie. I can't imagine what it was like for her to grow up as a television personality. She's actually somewhat of a hero to me for overcoming so much."

Steve said, "She's one of the most amazing young women you'll ever meet."

Heather immediately said, "Would you like to?"

"Like to what?"

"Meet Bella. She and her husband Adam are our next-door neighbors. We're having a double housewarming party this evening. Steve and I are moving into our new homes today."

"What a great idea," said Steve.

Stewart had followed Heather and was standing in the doorway. "You go, honey. Fred's had you cooped up all week. You're already dressed, and I'd like a firsthand report on Heather's development. It caused quite a stir among our neighbors. Some have already bought second homes with lake views."

Heather said, "I still have several available."

Fred spoke up. "I'm not sure this is a good idea on such short notice."

Steve took his turn. "I disagree. It's the perfect time because it's spontaneous. No one expects you and Lisa to go anywhere.

Besides, our new homes are on a gated peninsula with water on three sides and we have two exceptional dogs. The east side of the property has a twelve-foot metal fence, and the coded entry gate is the only dry way in. Le Roi and Heather's dog are the greeters for anyone who comes by boat."

Heather added. "I could ride with you and help watch for anyone trying to tail us."

Stewart had the last word. "Grab your purse and go, honey. We won't let them imprison us in our own home."

Once in the car, Rasheed asked, "A successful meeting?"

"Time will tell," said Steve. "And I hope time speaks sooner rather than later."

# Chapter Eighteen

Heather made frequent glances over her shoulder for the first several miles after leaving the Clay's home. She rode in the back seat of the Cadillac Escalade behind a man who looked as if he'd had all vestiges of mirth surgically removed. She thought how much Fred and the driver looked and acted alike. All business, all the time.

Heather relaxed, turned to Lisa, and made a mental list of her appearance to give to Steve. *Trophy wife, but wasn't born that way. Mid-to-late thirties but looks younger. Well educated, but not at elite schools. Likes the things money can buy. Manicured nails. Salon cut and styled hair with highlights. Has a personal trainer. Dentist brightens her teeth regularly.*

She took one more glance over her shoulder. "There's no use in me continuing to look for a tail. We'd have spotted one by now. How does it feel to be out in the world again?"

"Delightful, but not totally free. The extra precautions Stewart insists on make me feel like a caged bird."

"What was security like before Dan died?"

"Fred was the only constant. He's been watching after

Stewart for many years. He came to live at the house after a series of threats to Stewart's life. The first thing Fred did was beef up electronic surveillance. Then came the dogs who roam the grounds at night and the house during the day. Additional men came and went depending on how active the environmental protesters or other threats were."

"Did things change much when Dan ran for office?"

"Not at our home, except Stewart came close to firing Fred."

Heather shot a questioning look at Lisa.

"Fred warned my husband to get a team of bodyguards assigned to protect Dan. Dan didn't want them. Stewart listened to Dan instead of Fred, and now he doesn't have a son."

Lisa let out a sigh of regret. "Dan was busy playing the field. Fast cars, faster women, and old Scotch, if you know what I mean."

"He must have taken the divorce hard."

"He coped the same way my husband did with the death of his first wife. Work hard and play harder. I was the play part in his life."

Heather blew out a breath. "That must be why Stewart's drinking before noon."

"And smoking. He's grieving and blaming himself. After all, it's not like we didn't have money enough to pay for Dan's protection."

Heather moved on to something she thought would be more pleasant. "It shouldn't come as a surprise that Steve and I have done some research on you."

"I thought you might have after our talk in my office. Ask what you wish. My life is an open book."

"You were a nurse who took care of Stewart's first wife while she was battling cancer. Right?"

"A hospice nurse, but only for a few months with Patricia. I lived in the house with the family and slept in a daybed in Patricia's room. Twenty-four-seven for three months. It paid off my college loans." She turned to face Heather. "Dan was in college and Cindy was in the fourth grade. Nothing happened between me and Stewart for two years after he buried her. I moved out and kept working as an RN. Stewart remembered me and called me out of the blue." She paused. "That's what you really wanted to know."

Heather didn't have to tell her she was right. Her eyes had a piercing, knowing quality about them.

Lisa continued. "I'll give you more details. Stewart and I parted ways after I helped him find an au pair to replace me. We didn't speak for one year, eleven months and thirty days. It was the anniversary of Patricia's funeral that caused him to remember me. He invited me to accompany him to her grave, and I went. We talked about him moving on past grief and he said he was ready to. It surprised me when he said I was the one he wanted. We married in a civil ceremony three months later. Dan didn't care one way or the other if I was his stepmother. Cindy cried."

A rusty Dodge half-ton pickup blew a tire in front of them. The driver made a quick maneuver to avoid rear-ending the truck then sped up. The sound of screaming tires and metal twisting sounded behind them.

Heather leaned forward. "Nice job."

"Thanks. Nine years stock car racing pays off when driving in Houston."

Heather took out her phone.

Fred spoke from the front seat. "Who are you calling?"

"Fred," said Lisa. "Give it a rest. It's none of our business who's she calling."

"I don't mind," said Heather. "I'm calling the vet. Someone tried to poison my cat."

"That's horrible," said Lisa. "I hope he'll be all right." She altered her comment. "Or she."

"He," said Heather as she placed the call.

The call ended after Heather received assurance that Max was doing better than expected. The vet wanted to keep him overnight, but she could pick him up the next day, barring any complications.

"Good news?" asked Lisa.

"Excellent news."

"How was he poisoned?" asked Fred.

"Antifreeze. No one was home, including both dogs. Bella and Steve found him in time."

Fred voiced his opinion. "Some people don't deserve to live. I can't think of anything lower than trying to poison a pet."

"I can," said Lisa. "Bill Boyd killing my husband's son."

Heather pulled in a breath and put some sparkle into her voice. "We're crossing over the county line. No more talk about death. We're going to a celebration. You'll love Bella and Adam."

---

HEATHER SPOKE to Lisa's driver. "Get close to my car. The gate will stay open long enough for two cars to go through, but not three."

"What happens then?" asked Fred.

"Spike strips come up and trap you between the gate and forty yards beyond."

"That explains the guardrails on both sides. I like it. You trap the vehicle between the gate and four flat tires."

"It was Steve's idea. He wanted the rails to extend farther, but I thought fifty yards was too far. Of course, I can disable everything from my phone or inside my house."

"Is the cattle guard where the spike strips are?"

"That's correct."

"What are the circles on the driveway's surface on the other side of the cattle guard?"

"Reinforced concrete pillars that shoot up to form a last barrier. Steve wanted spikes. I wanted pillars. We got both."

"Smart."

"We know what it's like to be threatened."

Lisa looked out of her window. "The setting is stunning, and the precautions you've taken blend into the landscaping."

Heather said, "I detect a note of surprise in your voice. I'm guessing it's because I didn't build one large mansion instead of four single-level homes."

"Well, yes. They're very nice, but with your success..."

Heather let Lisa's words roll out until they stopped for lack of momentum. "The first home we're passing belongs to Bella's parents. Technically, it's a duplex, but the only thing they share with Adam and Bella is the four-car garage. We're all expecting children's toys in the yard after nature takes its course."

"Did you design your home with a big family in mind?"

Heather chuckled. "My maternal instinct is sorely lacking. In fact, it's practically non-existent."

She directed the conversation off herself. "Steve worked with my architect and Bella to design his home. He and his late wife never had children."

"I remember reading that in Bella's book. It's a shame Steve's wife died such a senseless death. Wasn't her name Maggie?"

Heather nodded. "Maggie was his one and only."

The pause was brief before Heather said, "As you can see, Steve and I also share a garage. We made one half of his garage into a home gym we'll share if we don't want to go to the community recreation center. Otherwise, his is a compact three-bedroom home with an office. That's one more bedroom than he's ever owned. I had to twist his arm to get him to agree to a third bedroom."

"How did you talk him into it?"

"I told him he needed to have a bedroom for the boy and girl Bella and Adam would provide."

The Escalade wheeled into the driveway, and Heather explained the extra vehicles for Fred's sake. "The minivan parked on Steve's side of the driveway belongs to Pam, my personal assistant. She supervised the move today. The caterers will be here about four."

"The view of the lake must be stunning from your backyard."

"It is, especially at sunset. I'm thinking about putting in an infinity pool before next spring. I'd like your opinion on the best location."

The car came to a stop, and the occupants piled out. Princess ran from her car in the garage to Heather's side and sat, waiting to receive her pat on the head. Steve and Le Roi joined them.

Heather watched as Fred turned to address the driver. "Check out everything on the outside."

"Hold on," said Steve. "We have a quicker way to do that." He instructed Le Roi in French to search to the right. Heather told Princess to do the same to the left. The dogs took off like they'd waited all day to run at full speed.

Heather turned to the driver. "You can go through the house, but don't get off the back patio unless Rasheed, Pam, or any of us who live this side of the fence are with you. Steve and my driver have done an excellent job in training the dogs to protect our little slice of heaven."

Lisa raised her eyebrows. "I'm dying to see your home. It feels so open and free compared to living in the city. The smell of the pines and the sound of boats on the lake make me long for a get-away. Would it be possible for us to tour the development later?"

"Absolutely. I'll give you the grand tour."

Fred said, "Our car and our driver."

"Of course," said Heather. "Princess will ride in the back. I have everything from condos and homes overlooking fairways to a few lakeside homes still available." Heather shifted her gaze. "What do you think, Fred?"

For the first time, he let his guard down. "I wouldn't mind living out here someday."

Lisa corrected him. "That's not what she meant. She wanted your opinion if it was safe enough to look at the development."

"Oh, yeah. Sure. It will be fine. It's a restricted community with armed security patrols. Heather and I are both armed, and the dog will be with us when we get out."

Heather asked, "Would you like to see our homes now, or tour the development?"

Lisa and Fred traded glances before she said, "I hope you don't think I'm rude, but I'd like to see the development. I've not pestered Stewart for anything new for a long time. I'm getting a terrible itch for a lake house."

"That settles it," said Heather. "Let's see if we can find something to help you scratch that itch."

# Chapter Nineteen

Heather looked out the kitchen window of her new home as the morning sun peeked through tall pine trees. Not a bad way to start the day, but life involved compromises, and a major one had been putting the kitchen and dining room on the front-facing side of her home. The decision maximized the number of other rooms with a view of the lake but resulted in a view of the front yard and future park from her kitchen window. She'd built a complete outdoor kitchen to help offset the disappointment of not being able to see water while making her morning coffee.

Steve called out as he came in through the garage door. His voice set Princess's tail to swinging. The click of Le Roi's nails on the travertine floor only increased its speed. Heather greeted her neighbors with a good morning for Steve and an ear rub for Le Roi.

"Did you sleep well in your new home?"

"Not really," said Steve through a yawn. "New surroundings meant unfamiliar sounds. Le Roi was in and out all night."

"The same with me on the poor night's sleep. Princess

154

patrolled inside and out, and Max wasn't there to cuddle against me."

"Don't forget to bring Max home today on your way back from Galveston. And speaking of Galveston, I forgot to ask what you did to get Cindy away from Claire Strobel."

"I didn't have to do anything. Fred told me Claire's in Copenhagen attending a climate conference. I called Cindy, told her I was checking on her and wanted to see her. She was much more talkative, and I'm set to meet her this morning at a coffee shop."

"That's interesting," said Steve. "Did she sound relieved that Claire wasn't around?"

"Very relieved."

Steve changed the conversation by saying, "The coffee's finished brewing. Is there a chance you could put some in a mug for me?"

"Sorry. It was a short night. I stayed up after everyone left and recorded my notes on our interviews with Stewart and Lisa."

"I hope you included Fred Lawrence."

"How could I forget him? He stuck to Lisa like wallpaper. Never let her out of his sight unless she went to powder her nose."

"I heard you talking to her about buying something out here. Is she serious?"

"Lisa fell in love with two homes I showed her. One on the lake and the other overlooking one of the golf courses. I think she would have signed a contract last night if she could have chosen between the two. Fred reminded her she needed to talk to her husband first. She asked Fred which one he preferred, and he chose the one overlooking the third fairway. The home is much bigger, but the lot isn't anything special. The lot on the lake is much larger, but slopes sharply to the water. The home is smaller and has a real outdoorsy vibe."

Heather kept talking. "What got Lisa more excited than the homes was meeting Bella. They must have talked for a solid hour. Bella even got Fred to join in the conversation."

"That's Bella. Never met a stranger and makes everyone feel like the most important person in the room."

Heather's phone dinged an alert for an incoming text. She looked at it and said, "Rasheed's on his way."

"When did you say he's moving?"

"His condo is almost complete. The carpenter is building extra bookshelves in his office. That and touch-up is all that's left."

"It will be handy to have him living so close."

The doorbell rang, and Heather went to answer it with Princess by her side. "That's Bella. I thought we'd stop and have breakfast on the way. Her to Houston and Rasheed and me to Galveston." She spoke over her shoulder. "Sorry. You're on your own today. There's plenty of leftovers from the party."

"As long as there's meat, bread, and cheese, I'm set."

Steve sat on a barstool sipping his coffee when Bella gave him her standard greeting of a firm hug and a kiss on his cheek. "Are you sure about not going with us today?"

"Yesterday was too much excitement for an old guy like me. I need to rest."

Bella dragged her hand across his shoulders. "That's a big fib. You might stay here, but you only pretend to rest when there's a case to solve."

Steve ran his finger around the rim of his coffee cup. "You're partially right. Unlike Heather, I didn't do my homework last night and dictate my report on yesterday's interviews. And speaking of that, I expect a report from you."

"Me? All I did was come to the party and talk to Lisa."

"Exactly," said Steve. "She's the stepmother of our victim. Heather and I need to know what you talked about."

"It was mostly about me, but we discussed playing golf and her modeling an outfit or two for the upcoming winter line."

Heather joined the conversation. "She's going to model for you? When?"

"Tomorrow. I told you I had a big photoshoot scheduled; I'll be in Houston all day. The woman I had scheduled for vests canceled and Lisa is the perfect age, shape, and size for the selections. Her bodyguard objected until I promised we'd crop her face from the photo. I hope he'll change his mind. She's very photogenic."

Steve interrupted. "Le Roi just beat me to the punch by nudging my leg. He heard the garage door open before I did, which means Rasheed is here."

"Greetings," said Rasheed as he entered through the garage. "To those going to Galveston, your *carrus* awaits."

"What's a *carrus*?" asked Bella.

"It's Latin for a wheeled vehicle."

Heather responded with, "It's way too early for Latin vocabulary lessons. Let's keep the words simple until after breakfast." She poured him a cup of coffee.

"Ah, a slug of Joe," said Rasheed. "All I need is a stinker to go with it and I'll be aces."

Steve kept a straight face while everyone else chuckled. "It's sinker, not stinker, and there are no donuts here unless you hid one in the pocket of your zoot suit. Did you watch another noir detective movie last night?"

"James Cagney was exceptional."

"Speaking of gangsters," said Steve. "I hope you and Rasheed are free the day after tomorrow."

"Where are we going?" asked Heather before her driver could try out more 1930's banter.

"You and I need to talk to Leonard Spears."

She shook her head, even though Steve couldn't see her. Her first word came out with extra emphasis. "*I* need to talk to Spears. You and Le Roi need to stay here. Bill Boyd is bound to be near him, and I bet you two haven't exchanged Christmas cards since you arrested him."

"I've taken that into consideration and we're both going, even though it's against my better judgment to include you."

Heather quirked her head to one side and tried not to grit her teeth. "What's that crack supposed to mean?"

Steve issued one of his trademark grins. "Just checking to see if you'd keep your emotions under control. It's bound to be a tense situation, and I'd prefer it if Leo didn't have to shoot anyone."

"You stinker, and I didn't mean sinker. I bet you haven't called Leo or Spears to set up the meeting. You tested me to see how I'd react."

"Guilty as charged."

Bella interrupted. "This may sound strange, but it's good to hear you two testing each other again."

Rasheed held up a palm and straightened his posture. "The grinding wheel against the blade produces sparks and creates sharp edges."

Steve said, "That's actually a decent proverb."

"Thank you, my friend. It reminds me of my cousin Abdul."

Bella asked, "Is he a philosopher, too?"

"Oh, no. He makes knives and has a hand tremor. Many sparks but only dull edges. A brother finishes his work, and another cousin sells the knives."

Steve said, "Rasheed, I challenge you to come up with six more proverbs based on knives, sparks, and shared labor. I'll expect them tomorrow morning."

"It's time to go," said Heather before Rasheed could reply.

She passed behind Steve's back and whispered, "You're still a stinker. He'll make up proverbs all the way to Galveston and back."

"We'll talk when you get back, Sparky."

The trip to Galveston began with Bella following them in her car. By the time they stopped at a French cafe in The Woodlands for breakfast, Heather had reached her limit of listening to Rasheed explore new proverbs. Something needed to change after breakfast.

The answer came to her halfway through her crêpes Suzette. Her gaze rested on Rasheed. "I'm going to put in my earbuds, listen to alpha waves, and clear my mind while you drive."

"Excellent," said Rasheed. "I prefer beta waves, but alphas are very good, too. Your decision to rest your mind will give me time to think instead of talk while I'm driving in heavy traffic."

Heather wondered if she'd fallen into one of Steve's little traps. Did he issue the challenge to Rasheed so he'd jabber all the way to Galveston, which would get on her nerves? If so, she'd have to come up with a solution, which she had.

Another test? Probably.

She cut off another bite of her crêpe and whispered, "That stinker. He got me again."

"What did you say?"

"Nothing. Just thinking out loud."

The weather and traffic cooperated, and with her mind shifting into neutral, time passed quickly. So fast, it surprised her to be looking down at Galveston Bay from the top of the bridge that connected mainland Texas to the island.

She took out her earbuds and stored them in their case. She might have been looking at multiple boats of all descriptions and sizes, but her thoughts zeroed in on Cindy Clay and what she would ask the timid woman.

Rasheed asked, "Do you want me to stay in the car with Princess while you conduct your interview?"

Heather talked her way through an answer to the question. "Cindy impressed me as being very cautious around strangers. I'm not sure how she'll react to you. The coffee shop overlooks the gulf, across the street from the seawall." Before Rasheed could ask, she explained, "The seawall is a wide, curved concrete barrier meant to prevent destruction of the island from hurricanes. It's topped with a sidewalk overlooking the beach. With today's clouds and the onshore breeze, it would be a great day for you to take a long walk."

"Say no more. I have a pen and a notebook. The wind and waves will inspire me to write several proverbs while Princess calms the timid lady, and you pump the broad for the down low."

"It's lowdown," said Heather as she tried not to laugh. "I wouldn't recommend calling women broads. It's a good way to get a smack across the chops, a shiner, and a fat lip. That doesn't include getting pumped full of lead by a crazy dame with a gat."

Rasheed's smile stretched across his face. "American-gangster is a most fascinating language."

The trip through the long, narrow island didn't take long. Squawks from seagulls greeted her as soon as she opened her door, as did heavy, moist air, fresh from the spray of curling waves. Only a few more steps and she and Princess would meet with Cindy... unless the timid woman had changed her mind and stiffed her.

# Chapter Twenty

Heather shouldn't have wasted a perfectly good worry on Cindy not meeting her. The young woman sat at a window table and displayed a wide smile when she saw the dog wearing her service vest.

"Good morning," said Heather as she handed the leash to Cindy. "You look like a dog lover. I hope you don't mind if I leave her here while I get a mocha latte. She's very well-behaved and won't leave you unless I tell her to. Her name is Princess."

Cindy's eyes came alive, as did her voice, but in a soft volume. "I don't mind a bit. I love animals of all kinds. Dogs are my favorite, but, unfortunately, I can't keep one in my condo." Her face darkened. "I used to have cats, but they kept running away."

Heather's thoughts turned to Max. "I have a cat that's big enough to be two. He's in the kitty hospital recovering from someone poisoning him."

Cindy's eyes sparked with anger. "There's no punishment bad enough for someone like that."

"Show love," said Heather to her dog. Princess responded by putting her head in Cindy's lap. The stroking began immediately and Heather knew she'd played an ace and won the first hand. Princess had broken the ice of what might have been an awkward opening to the meeting. After all, the last time they met, Cindy was in a hospital bed and Heather and Bella were told to leave.

The barista worked her magic and Heather returned with a white paper cup filled with caffeinated joy and steam shooting from the small opening in the lid.

Instead of jumping into a conversation, Heather waited to see if Cindy would initiate one. Over the years, Steve had drilled into her the under-appreciated value of silence.

Cindy dipped her head. "I want to start by apologizing. Claire was very rude to you and Bella. I told her so, but that's just the way Claire is."

"It's nothing," said Heather. "Among other things, I'm an attorney and originally from Boston. People there are born with thick skin, especially those who get paid to confront others."

Cindy countered with, "I could tell what Claire said didn't bother you, but I think it hurt Bella. I wish you could have stayed longer. Were you visiting other hospital patients?"

"Only you. My dad knows your father."

A note of longing entered Cindy's simple response of, "It's been a long time since I've spoken with my father."

Heather tilted her head. "We have more in common than you realize."

"How's that?"

"My father and I had a lousy relationship when I was growing up. He had little to do with me from the moment I was born. He worked almost constantly and also expected my mother to be a fixture in Boston's upper crust. The good news is, my father and I reconciled and now enjoy each other's company."

Cindy cast her gaze to the gulf and spoke with self-pity. "My father hates me. I'm nothing but a disappointment to him."

"I used to think the same thing. Of course, my rebelling didn't help." Heather leaned into Cindy and spoke in a conspiratorial manner. "Do you know what I did to drive him away?"

Cindy closed the distance. "What?"

"I quit taking money from him, became a cop in Boston, and worked my way through law school without his help. They were the hardest years of my life, but I was idealistic and determined to make the world a better place to live."

"That's what I'm trying to do, but differently. How long were you a cop?"

"Ten years. My father had the political connections to get me fired from the police force, so I fled to Texas and tried to start over with Houston PD. His influence reached across state lines. That's when two things happened that changed my life and my way of thinking."

Heather knew she had Cindy hooked into her story and it was time to reel her in, so she delayed by taking a few sips of coffee.

"You've got me on the edge of my seat. What two things?"

"First, a brilliant former homicide cop needed a partner to help him solve a murder, and we became private detectives."

Heather went back to the coffee to increase Cindy's curiosity. It didn't take long. "What's the second thing?"

"I received a large inheritance from my grandparents and started my own investment company. It turns out I have my father's ability to create businesses or make other businesses more profitable. That means more jobs in the US and around the world."

"I hope they're green jobs, not like my father's."

Heather didn't want to go down a rabbit trail that led to contention, so she shifted back to her story. "This week, I'm taking a break from business so I can work with my detective partner to solve a murder. Your brother's."

The gasp that came from Cindy was loud enough to cause people at nearby tables to turn and look. Heather covered Cindy's right hand with her left and increased the pace of her words. "That's why Bella and I came to see you. She sometimes helps with our investigations."

"She's the most beautiful woman I've ever met, and so kind."

"Bella and her husband, Adam, are my next-door neighbors."

"Wow! How lucky you are."

Heather needed to get back on track, so she revisited her coffee, set the cup on the table and asked, "I'm thinking your assault could be connected to Dan's murder. Are you still in danger?"

Cindy responded with a firm shake of her head.

"That's good to know," said Heather. "Your father will be relieved to hear it."

"My father?" Her eyes darted back and forth. "Did he send you?"

"No, but my partner and I interviewed him yesterday, and he's worried about you. I could tell."

"How?"

"My partner told me he still gives you money. That's how my father showed me he cared, until I refused to take any more."

Cindy's words came out slowly. "I see what you mean. He lets me live in a condo he bought years ago. It's down the street, overlooking the gulf."

"Do you live alone?"

"Not really."

Heather lifted her eyebrows to get her to explain. "It's a four bedroom. Claire has a room, but she spends more than half her time traveling to conferences, events, and protests. She schedules others in the movement to stay in the condo when there's a local protest. They come from all over and leave after the event or when they get out of jail."

"How have you avoided being arrested?"

A shrug of her shoulders was a partial answer. "I don't stay long at the events. Claire arranges a quick television interview for me and then I go home. She tells me I'm more valuable doing other things. In case you haven't noticed, I'm neither assertive nor attractive."

"I believe every woman is beautiful. Of course, a day at a salon never hurt any of us.," Heather smiled at the young woman.

Cindy's eyes danced with excitement, but the joy left faster than it came. "Thanks, but most cosmetics are made from petroleum products."

"A salon is not all about cosmetics," said Heather. "A facial is one of the simplest things you can do to enhance your natural beauty. As for cosmetics, I read the label and pick those that are petroleum free, organic, or natural. Bella does, too."

"Claire says you can't trust the labels."

Heather wasn't there to debate, so she simply smiled and asked, "Does your father give you an allowance?"

"Sort of. I have a debit card with a monthly limit on it. Most of the time, it's enough to take care of groceries. It all depends on how many people stay at the condo. I also work to fill in the gaps."

"Where do you work?"

"It's like a food truck; except I sell natural honey and vanilla from Mexico."

"How much do you make?"

"I don't get paid directly. I save Claire from having to hire someone. She makes up the difference if I run short of food."

A clear picture of Claire Strobel emerged, and it wasn't pretty. Instead of telling Cindy she was a fool for allowing herself to be Claire's doormat, Heather refocused on Dan's murder. "Do you have any theories about who killed Dan and why?"

"My guess is it's related to the oil business and greed, probably someone poisoning the air and water so they can increase profits. You know, something to do with big business."

"Did Claire tell you that?"

"Uh-huh. She's real smart about those things."

"What about the political angle? Could it have anything to do with your brother unseating an incumbent in the last election?"

A blank look came over Cindy's face. "We vote for whoever is running from the Green Party. In this part of Texas, it doesn't take long to vote. There are never many green candidates on the ballot."

Heather took several more sips of coffee and changed the subject completely. "I owe you an apology. I haven't asked about your injuries."

Cindy flipped the question off with her hand like it was a pesky gnat. She couldn't, however, look Heather in the eyes as she said, "Only a few stitches and bruises. Nothing to worry about. I'm not going out at night alone and I'm making sure the doors stay locked. It was just one of those things that happens on Galveston Island."

Heather detected deception again. Galveston was like any large city, with its share of crime. Perhaps more on the island because it attracted so many visitors. What wasn't normal was an assault, a knifing, and a gunshot happening to one woman at the same time. Even more puzzling, the injuries were all superficial. Her first inclination was to believe Claire Strobel did it to keep Cindy in line. Perhaps she did, but why go to the trouble of using all three? She wondered what Steve would say.

It surprised Heather when Cindy asked, "How was my father's health when you saw him yesterday?"

She chose not to sugarcoat the response. "Mentally, he's grieving deeply, and this is affecting him physically."

"Is he drinking too much again?"

"We arrived well before noon, but he was drinking Scotch on the rocks."

"Johnny Walker Blue Label will be the death of him. That and cigarettes. Smoking and air pollution from the refineries is what killed my mother." She corrected herself. "Not the booze. Mom drank in moderation. Her death is what got me interested in environmental studies."

"There's something else you need to know," said Heather. "Your father has turned his home and grounds into an armed camp. He believes whoever killed your brother will come for him or your stepmom next."

Fear came into her eyes. "Has he taken adequate precautions?"

"It's a fortress with dogs and human guards."

"How ironic. He never allowed me to have a dog after he remarried. My stepmother didn't like them." She continued to stroke Princess.

Heather allowed several seconds to pass before she said, "Speaking of your stepmother, how did you two get along?"

Cindy extended her hand and wiggled it. "Not good, not bad. She was more like an older sister who was arm decoration for Dad. She wasn't interested in me. I have to admit, she's still a hot-looking woman. I see her picture in the paper now and then."

"You and she have something in common."

"No way," said Cindy with extra emphasis.

"You're both Bella admirers. She and her bodyguard came to the lake yesterday to meet her."

"What lake?"

"Lake Conroe. I had a housewarming party. Lisa was so excited to talk to Bella that she's considering buying a second home close to where Bella and her husband live."

"That sounds like something Lisa would do, and my father won't hesitate to pull out his checkbook to make her happy."

Cindy hurled out a breath and pinched her eyebrows together.

Heather didn't know for sure the reason for the sudden change of expression but had an idea about what Cindy was thinking. "Are you worried about your dad?"

"Some, but that's not what I was thinking about. I imagined what it would be like to live in a place with clean air and fresh water instead of what flows out of the ship channel, into the bay, and washes onto shore. You know, I'm imagining a place to live where tall trees breathe in carbon dioxide and breathe out oxygen. A place where the air and ground smell like they should."

"You should visit me. I insisted on leaving as many trees as possible in the development and we're close to Sam Houston National Forrest."

Cindy looked out the window. "I wish I could."

Heather took a chance with her next words. "You're deeply involved with environmental activists. One theory concerning your brother's death is activists could be involved. Do you think that's possible?"

Cindy surprised her with her answer. "I've wondered the

same thing. They usually draw the line at human roadblocks, defacing property, and other forms of mostly peaceful protests."

"Aren't there some who advocate escalating things?"

She nodded.

"Does Claire Strobel want more done?"

Cindy nodded again.

Heather let the issue rest without pushing Cindy to say more.

"I need to get to work," said Cindy. "There's a quota of sales I'm required to meet."

"Can I give you a lift?" asked Heather.

"I only ride my electric bike, but thanks anyway."

"Any time you want to visit the lake, I'll come get you."

"Thanks, but I don't see that happening anytime soon."

"Do you want me to tell your father anything?"

Cindy hesitated, looking for words that seemed stuck between her heart and her tongue. She finally said, "I guess not."

Heather picked up the leash from the floor, cleared the table, and threw her trash away. Cindy stopped on the sidewalk outside and bent down to give Princess a final hug. She then turned and ran in the opposite direction, where a chain held her bicycle firmly against a street sign.

Rasheed appeared and said, "I have the car cooling. I'll put Princess in her cell if you're ready to leave."

"I'm more than ready."

Rasheed waited until they were rolling before he asked, "Was it a successful interview?"

"Successful but terribly depressing."

"Mine was depressing, too. My muse didn't like the smell of dead fish. There were several that floated ashore. I wonder if there was a spill of something that killed them."

"That's possible. Let's go home."

# Chapter Twenty-One

T he trip from Galveston to Heather's new lakeside home passed relatively quickly because Rasheed pulled her out of the funk that clung to her after speaking with Cindy. He waited until they reached the mainland before saying. "Your countenance is downcast."

That was all it took to get her to talking. "I don't like bullies."

"Ah," said Rasheed. "You have touched on a subject I have much experience with. The desire for control is present in almost all people. It is the motive behind the desire that separates the kind from the cruel, the giver from the taker, the sacrificer from the sadist. It is fortunate that most people lean more toward good than bad."

Heather shot him a glance. "Do you really believe that?"

He answered with a simple statement. "You challenge me with a question. Very well. Yes, I believe there is more good in most people than evil."

Heather challenged him again. "But only most people. Not all."

"There are more sheep than wolves and they need protecting. I deduce from your reaction after today's interview that Cindy Clay is a lamb in danger."

"That's very perceptive of you, but what if she helped a wolf kill a fellow sheep?"

"You and Steve are shepherds. You know how to deal with wolves."

Heather looked out her window at a distant refinery. "I'd like to pull their teeth out."

"Or, rub 'em out with a Tommy gun."

Heather spoke through a laugh. "Steve wouldn't approve of either. I'll need to be more inventive."

The ride home continued with many miles passing without words, but her thoughts focused on Cindy and other victims of predators. How many wolves had she arrested as a cop? How many bullies had she fired from her own company? It was a shame Claire Strobel didn't work for her. She'd derive great pleasure in telling Claire to pack her personal items and leave immediately. A security guard would make sure she didn't dally.

Heather's thoughts turned to her cat. "Don't forget, we need to pick up Max on the way home."

"How could one forget such a fine animal? He will be overjoyed to see you. If pet hospitals are anything like hospitals for humans, he will have found the food displeasing."

"No doubt. That goes for the quality and quantity. Steve is such a sucker when Max begs for things he shouldn't have."

Rasheed then asked, "Are you sure Bucky Franklin poisoned him?"

"Who else hates me or Steve enough to do such a thing?"

"Only you, Steve, and possibly Leo can answer that question. I'm wondering if you have."

Heather asked, "Have what?"

171

"Ruled out everyone else as a suspect. The world's greatest detective once said, and I paraphrase, 'After you've ruled out all other possibilities, whoever remains is the person you seek.'"

"I've heard different variations of that same idea. It has limitations, namely a lack of hard evidence. There were no fingerprints on the bowl that held the antifreeze. The lock on the gate was missing and wasn't found. That tells me the person was meticulous enough to take it with them to dispose of. Police reports said our closest neighbors were at work and none had exterior cameras. Whoever poisoned Max stayed out of view until they spray-painted the camera lens of our security camera."

Heather let out a huff. "All that adds up to a big zero in the evidence column. When that happens, dig deeper for evidence until you're convinced there is none."

"Then the detective gives up?" asked Rasheed.

"No. That's when you interview suspects and get very creative with your questions."

"Ah-hah! The old third degree. Rubber hoses to the torso and bright lights until the guy breaks."

"That's the general idea," said Heather, "but without the lights, hoses, cattle prods, lead-filled slappers, or brass knuckles. Nothing but questions."

"Do you mind if we change the subject?" asked Rasheed. "Your list of enhanced interview techniques brought back many dark memories. Perhaps I should watch different movies at night."

"Or you could read," said Heather.

"An excellent suggestion, and that's how I spend much of my time. My duties at the office are light and flexible, as is my primary job of driving you and Steve wherever you desire to go."

Heather turned to face him. "That's only partially true. My

father also pays you to spy on me. You and Steve both report to him." She put up a hand. "Don't deny it, and I think it's wonderful that he cares so much about me and the future of his company."

"His company?" asked Rasheed in a bewildered tone.

"Of course. My father is a master in business strategy. My mental breakdown and continuing recovery have his well-laid plans for the future in jeopardy. He needs constant reassurance that I'm getting progressively better. He trusts you and Steve to confirm my progress."

She could see her father sitting behind his desk, deep in thought. "My dad is at the age when men like him spend more and more time thinking about what will happen when they're gone."

"Your father loves you intensely," said Rasheed.

"I know that's true, but he also loves his business. The two are not mutually exclusive."

"Well said. People have many loves. Most come and go like seasons, but some live with them until the end."

"Like Steve and his late wife, Maggie?"

Rasheed allowed several seconds to pass. "I cannot deny that Maggie remains in his heart and will live there until he dies. However, I sense companionship in Steve's future." He shot her a quick glance. "I could be wrong."

"I hope you're right," said Heather as a smile pulled up the corners of her mouth. "And speaking of companionship, how are things between you and Junani?"

"Frustrating. Doris, the de facto leader of the third floor, along with Pam, your personal assistant, secured replacement clothing for the business suit ruined during the car chase. I'm waiting for a free day to deliver them to Junani."

Heather didn't hesitate. "It won't be long before we arrive at my home. Steve will want a full report of my visit with

Cindy Clay. He and I will discuss our strategy for tomorrow when we meet with Leonard Spears."

Rasheed drummed his fingers on the steering wheel. "Another day's delay in completing my task of delivering the garment to Junani."

"Nonsense. Steve and I will remain at home for the rest of the afternoon and tonight. Your assignment is to call Junani and meet her tonight with the package and flowers. You are to take her to dinner at the restaurant of your choice and confirm whether she wants to proceed with becoming a member of our legal team. If she does, her next interview will be with the head of that department." She took a breath. "Questions?"

"My brain and tongue are no longer connected."

---

LE ROI MET HEATHER, Princess, and Rasheed in the garage with chin up and a wagging tail. He then went back through the oversized pet door and awaited the arrival. Rasheed backed out of the garage, and the door lowered.

After freeing Max from his cage and putting out fresh food and water for him, she found Steve in his recliner with feet up. Heather knew for sure he wasn't asleep when he asked, "I heard Rasheed leave. Where's he going?"

"To find true love," said Heather.

"I wish him luck with getting his tongue untied."

Heather settled into a chair matching the one Steve sat in. "How do you like having more room?"

"Still getting used to it. This is the largest home I've ever lived in and it's just me and Le Roi. In a way, it seems like a waste of space."

"Was your home with Maggie smaller?"

"Maggie loved the craftsman style homes, and we found

one that needed work. It was three bedrooms that we hoped to fill with kids. We used what would have been the nursery as her art studio and the second bedroom for guests and storage—mainly storage."

Heather changed the subject. "You look comfortable. Did I catch you taking a nap?"

"Not today. I save those for days when we don't have a killer to catch. Tell me about your interview with Cindy Clay."

"I got a good read on her and came away with an even lower opinion of Claire Strobel."

"Do you need something to eat or drink before you give me the details?"

"I'll fix us both a plate of leftover sandwiches if you haven't eaten."

"That would be wonderful. There are bottles of cold water, too."

Heather rose and went to the kitchen. "Come sit at the bar so I don't have to holler."

Steve, Le Roi, and Princess followed her. He then asked, "Where's Max?"

"Exploring his new home. He's glad to be rid of the collar of shame, but I thought it best to let him explore our house first. I'm sure he'll make his way over here before long."

Heather opened the door to the refrigerator. "There's a platter of Hawaiian rolls stuffed with an assortment of meats with cheeses."

"Give me three. It doesn't matter what kind."

"What about baby carrots, celery sticks, cherry tomatoes, and dip?"

"Sure. Anything that I can eat fast and not make much of a mess."

"The same for me," said Heather. "Do you want me to give

175

you a report while I fix your plate and we eat, or would you rather wait?"

"Let's multi-task. Start with the trip to Galveston and go heavy on the details when you get to the interview with Cindy."

Steve chuckled when she told him how she used earbuds to block out Rasheed's voice as he talked his way through developing new proverbs. He also nodded his approval when she used Princess to gain Cindy's trust.

He interrupted her narrative and said, "She must be a true animal lover. Would you say she's more passionate about animals or the environment?"

She pursed her lips together for a few seconds. "I assumed it was the environment, but she never stopped petting Princess. I haven't gotten to the part of the story where she said she longs for a dog, but Claire won't hear of it."

Steve jumped in. "I think I know why. During a climate protest in Germany, the police used dogs to help disperse the crowd. Claire learned the hard way not to spray police officers with paint. A dog mauled her."

Heather continued her narrative and finished her lone roast beef and cheese mini-sandwich long after Steve wiped his mouth with a paper towel.

"Let's go back to the living room," said Steve. "You've given me lots of things to consider. I'll do the dishes later."

"In other words, you'll put the paper plates and plastic bottles in the recycle bin."

He didn't respond, only slid off the barstool and walked to his recliner. She cleared the bar and joined him.

The footrest came up with a push of a button, but Steve kept the back in an upright position. "Do you believe Cindy Clay assisted Claire Strobel in luring her brother to the reflecting pool at the San Jacinto Monument?"

Heather puffed out her cheeks and released a breath. "Not knowingly, but that doesn't mean Claire didn't bully or trick her into it."

She turned the question around for him to answer it. He responded with, "I had Leo do more research on Claire. You're not the only one with contacts at the FBI. Claire's well known at the Bureau. She flies frequently, in business class no less."

"Upscale hotels?" asked Heather.

"Especially in Europe."

"That's all good information," said Heather, "But my sources told me Claire was out of the country when someone killed Dan."

"Have you looked at Claire's arrest record?"

"Of course. No arrests in the last two years."

"Exactly," said Steve. "She's moved up in the organization to the point she's too valuable to them to spend time in jail."

Heather rose from her chair and gave him an accusatory stare. "You're up to something. What is it?"

"Nothing yet, but I'll let you know when it's fully thought out. In the meantime, we need to talk about our meeting tomorrow with Leonard Spears."

"Is Leo going?"

"Nope. Just me, you, and Le Roi."

"What about Princess?"

"She stays in the car again. You may need to get to your pistol in a hurry. If so, I don't want her yanking the leash and making you miss your shot."

"Why can't Leo go, too?"

"Spears won't talk to us if there's anyone with a badge with us. It was the best deal I could make. Leo will be nearby, along with plenty of help."

"I don't like it," said Heather.

"Me either, but we're trying to prevent a war, not take part in one."

Heather imagined how the meeting would begin. "I don't want to be searched."

"You will be, but only with a wand. No touching allowed."

"Wait a minute," said Heather. "How do you expect me to be armed if they search me with a metal- detecting wand?"

"I'm expecting a delivery tonight from an old acquaintance."

Heather scowled, even though Steve couldn't see her. "Every time you use the word *acquaintance*, it turns out to be an ex-con that owes you a favor."

Steve ignored her observation. "He's bringing a pistol with no metal parts. I'm pretty sure he said it's made of ceramic."

"And illegal. I could go to prison for possessing one of those, let alone using it."

Steve shrugged. "Then don't use it unless absolutely necessary. We're going to talk, not shoot."

Heather had her mouth open to give another objection when Steve said, "I'm interested to hear where you'll hide it so you'll have quick access, but they can't see it."

Heather threw up her hands. "The pistol goes back after tomorrow."

"I'll keep it in my house," said Steve. "You might need it again."

# Chapter Twenty-Two

Deep feline purrs brought Heather out of her slumber as dim daylight shone through her bedroom window. She looked down at the black ball of fur that lay contoured to her body. "Good morning, my handsome bed buddy." She gave Max a head scratch, and he rolled over on his back and flexed his claws on all four feet.

A quick glance at the floor brought questions she put words to. "Where's Princess? Did she go outside?"

The cat's only response was to yawn and roll over.

"Time to get up, sleepy head. I have a busy day. The very first thing I want us to do is go on the back patio and look at the lake."

She threw back the covers and spoke again to Max. "You go to your litter box, I'll go to mine, and I'll see you outside."

It came as a bit of surprise when Heather smelled fresh-brewed coffee as she left her bedroom. She stopped by the kitchen, poured herself a serving in her favorite mug, and made for the patio door. She opened it and saw the back of Steve's head over the all-weather cushion on a rocking chair.

"Good morning," said Steve with a chipper voice. "Did you sleep better on your second night in your new house?"

Heather eased herself down into a matching rocker. "Tons better. Max made all the difference. We were like two spoons in a drawer. How about you? Still hearing strange noises?"

"Le Roi did. There was some sort of critter in the yard. I think he killed it."

"I hope it wasn't a neighborhood cat or a loose dog."

"Probably a field mouse or possibly an opossum. We'd know if it was a skunk."

Heather surveyed the area between their homes and the water. "I don't see anything in your backyard or mine."

"Check Bella and Adam's after you finish your coffee. The sound came from there last night."

Heather said, "I'd better look now. Bella's as soft-hearted about animals as Cindy Clay is. I'd hate for her to find what's left of a Fluffy or Fido."

Heather slipped her feet into a pair of Crocs and set out on a quest to find what was left of Le Roi's late-night vigilance. She saw nothing in Steve's yard, nor Bella and Adam's. She kept going into the backyard of Bella's parents' home. After examining the crime scene, she returned to her patio.

"Find anything?" asked Steve.

Heather settled back into her chair. "Yeah. Your dog killed an armadillo. He bit right through the armor."

Steve reached over and gave Le Roi a pat on the head. "Good boy. Armadillos can carry rabies and the bacteria that causes leprosy. They also dig up yards. On the positive side, they eat some insects you don't want in your lawn. I'll send Adam a text in a while and tell him to bury it."

"What about Le Roi? Do you need to take him to the vet?"

"Nah," said Steve in a nonchalant tone. "The vet would tell

you to watch him for a few days. The chances of the dog getting sick are very slim."

"I didn't know you were such an expert on armadillos."

"A buddy and I went hunting in Central Texas when I was a freshman in high school. We didn't see a single deer, but he killed an armadillo with a .22. It was the nastiest thing I ever cleaned. Getting it out of the shell was a fight."

Heather shook from her head down. "Please tell me you didn't eat it."

"It tasted pretty good after we cooked it over a campfire. Kind of like chicken." He quickly added, "That was before we learned the dangers. I'd never eat it again."

Heather rose. "I'd ask if that was another of your tall tales about what you did as a teen, but I'm afraid it's true."

"I'll give you my friend's name and number if you want to call him."

Heather shook her head and walked to the door. "No more talk of eating prehistoric creatures. I'm getting a fresh cup of coffee and looking at the lake for the next thirty minutes."

"Do you want to hear about a fishing trip my sophomore year in high school?"

"No. You probably caught a whale and ate it, too."

He hollered at her before she could slide the door to. "It was only a shark... a great white."

She dumped half a cup of cool coffee into the sink and refilled her cup with fresh. The smile left her face. "Steve's worried about the interview this afternoon. He always covers his anxiety by recalling things he did growing up or when he had his sight."

HEATHER WORKED from home as the hours passed before it was time to leave for Houston. Steve left after he admitted the shark he caught in high school was only a foot long. He also confessed to being scared when he removed the hook. The armadillo story, however, was mostly true. The few bites of badly burned meat tasted more like charcoal than chicken.

Rasheed arrived at one o'clock with slumped shoulders and a downcast gaze. "Good afternoon," he said, in a way that sounded like he'd lost his last friend.

Steve picked up on the despondent tone of his two-word greeting. "Let me guess," said Steve. "The meeting with Junani didn't turn out well."

Rasheed groaned. "I accomplished the task assigned to deliver the new clothes and flowers. We went to supper at a restaurant Doris recommended. Conversation started slowly for both of us. The room was dim and the candlelight on our table made her face look like that of a goddess. Her eyes shone like new copper pennies. We ordered, and the conversation picked up. I shared things about my family, and she did the same with hers. The food came, and we talked much and ate sparingly, even though the meal was superb. She ran many miles that morning and drank much water to rehydrate. Midway through the meal, she excused herself. I rose to help with her chair. That's when I committed an unforgivable sin."

"I doubt it was unforgivable," said Heather.

"I was so distracted by her beauty when we sat that I tucked the tablecloth under my belt. I must have thought it was my napkin."

Heather could see in her mind what was about to happen but allowed Rasheed to finish his story.

"I rose to help her with her chair. The tablecloth jerked everything on the table. I panicked and tried to grab the table but misjudged and pushed it instead. Half a bowl of ratatouille landed in her lap. Upside down, of course."

Rasheed wasn't finished. "I was harrified."

"That's horrified," said Steve.

"I was both, and alongside myself with shame."

This time, Steve didn't correct him.

"I hoped to clean her dress with the napkin in my hand. I shot to her side of the table, but I failed to pull the tablecloth out of my pants. Everything on the table ended up on the floor, but all I could think about was the stain. I reached for the spot on her dress where the stew had landed. It was in a most unfortunate location."

He closed his eyes and let out a mournful sigh. "I wiped once, and she slapped me. She's an excellent slapper. The patrons in the room cheered for her as she ran for the bathroom."

Steve asked, "How was the ride home?"

"Lonely. I was so ashamed of myself, I gave the manager extra for the mess I'd created, and gave him even more to apologize for me, and enough to pay for an Uber to take her home."

Heather asked, "Did you call her to apologize today?"

"My shame is too great."

"Can you still drive us to Houston today, or does Heather need to?" asked Steve.

"I need to focus on something other than my ineptitude, but please don't ask me to eat at a restaurant that has white tablecloths. I think PTSD would overtake me."

Heather's phone rang as she slipped the strap of her purse over her shoulder. It contained an empty compartment designed to carry a medium-size handgun, but the pistol Steve provided was a slim-line semi-automatic in a special holster that fit in the waistband of skinny jeans. Once covered by a loose-fitting cotton blouse and a linen jacket, the slight bulge disappeared.

After looking at the name on caller ID, she spoke so Steve could hear her. "This could be interesting. It's Lisa Clay."

Heather engaged the phone, making sure the speaker was on. "Hello, Lisa. Is everything all right?"

"Better than all right. I had to make a compromise, but I got Stewart to agree to purchase a weekend get-away in your development. It's the one on the lake with more trees."

"That's wonderful. Does Stewart want to take a tour of the home before making a final decision?"

"I took pictures of both properties. Stewart looked at them and his business mind took over. He said he could buy a home on a golf course anywhere. Lakefront property is where the biggest appreciation will take place. Because it's a golf cart community, we can enjoy the early mornings and afternoons looking at the lake, plus we can play golf whenever we want."

Lisa sucked in a quick breath and continued, "Once Stewart decides to purchase something, there's no stopping him. How soon before we can complete the deal?"

"The fastest way is for this to be a cash deal with all inspections waived. I can call my sales manager and have her get started on the paperwork."

Steve held up a hand, showing two fingers. He mouthed the words *two more days*. He then pointed to her and back to him twice.

Heather turned her attention back to Lisa. "If you agree on the listed price, no inspections, you don't want a new survey, and agree to take the home and lot, as is, I'll come to your home with the keys and contract the day after tomorrow. I'll need a check for the full amount. Whose name do you want on the contract?"

"Stewart's company. He said he could use it as a tax write off."

"This might be the easiest sale I ever made," said Heather. "By the way, how did the photo shoot go with Bella?"

"Fabulous. No, beyond fabulous," said Lisa. "Every time I meet Bella, she hugs me like she's known me all her life. She's an absolute doll. Her makeup artist worked magic, and the photographer knew every trick in the book."

"I'm glad it was such an enjoyable experience for you."

They exchanged a few parting words before Heather put her phone back in her purse.

Steve rose from a barstool. "A few million here, a few million there, and pretty soon you'll earn some real money."

Heather chewed the inside of her bottom lip. "I'm always nervous when deals go that smoothly."

Rasheed said, "Easy money wears track shoes."

Steve spoke over his shoulder. "Not bad, but the best parables have two stanzas."

# Chapter Twenty-Three

The trip from Montgomery County into Harris County took them past the airport and the location of Houston's police academy. Conversation was sparse and short-lived. Each human occupant, Heather, Steve, and Rasheed, seemed content to stay in their own thoughts.

They took the 610 Loop to the east again. Their destination was a warehouse near Houston's ship channel. As usual, large trucks filled most of the lanes instead of cars. Rasheed navigated around them with great skill, leaving Heather's mind free to consider whether Steve's plan was brilliant or a fool's folly. They'd discussed it the preceding night, but this was a plan that, in her opinion, relied on cunning and luck. She could see how the day might end badly for everyone concerned, especially her. Her trust in Steve would need to rise to a level that would test her nerve.

After winding their way through a labyrinth of decaying streets, they arrived at their destination, or at least the place the computer told them was their destination. The tin building was streaked with rust the color of dried blood and surrounded by a

186

ten-foot-tall chain-link fence topped with barbed wire. The sign on the gate read: BEWARE: DOGS ON PATROL AFTER CLOSING.

Rasheed looked at the words and said, "That sign would be better if they gave a closing time."

"What does it say?" asked Steve.

Heather told him, and he placed a hand on Rasheed's shoulder. "It's meant to convey the message that you're taking chances by entering. Closing time is whenever they want it to be."

A wall of a man with a craggy face walked from the building to the gate. He opened it and swung one side open. A thick hand motioned them in and a second man, not as large, came out of the building and pointed to the spot Rasheed was to park.

"You stay in the car with Princess," said Steve to Rasheed.

Heather exited the front seat on the passenger side as Steve climbed out of the back seat and unfurled his white cane. They went to the back of the SUV as the door swung open. "Le Roi, come," said Steve as Heather commanded Princess to stay.

Craggy Face closed the gate and secured it with a thick chain and a padlock. Steve took hold of the lead's handle and waited with Le Roi at his side. A second man carrying an AK-47 appeared from behind a pile of pallets. He seemed to lack a working vocabulary and pointed the rifle at a metal door with glass in a small window.

Heather led the way and stopped at the door. She saw the faint shape of a man's face appear in the window. The door opened and a man's squeaky voice instructed them to enter. They did, and Le Roi bared his teeth and growled. Steve gripped the harness and told Le Roi to heel and remain quiet. He obeyed but quivered with nervous energy. He knew what firearms were and didn't like people he didn't know being around Steve and Heather. Fortunately, the man stood well back but watched with his rifle at the ready.

She recognized the man giving orders from the picture in the file, but Heather didn't let on that she knew his life story. He wasn't tall or well built. The pock-marked face, almost certainly the result of untreated teenage acne, made her doubt he had pleasant years as an adolescent.

"Move to the table. Both of you. Empty your pockets, leave the purse, and back away."

They complied, but the man gave Heather an additional instruction. "Take the blazer off and leave it."

She shot him a quick glare but did as instructed.

Steve said, "I can leave my cane if you want to look at it, too. Be sure to check it carefully. I may have rigged it to fire a guided missile, or it could be a flame-thrower."

"You never were funny, Smiley." His voice cracked. "Yeah. Leave it. I'll try to remember to give it back to you."

Steve asked, "Bill Boyd? Is that you?"

"Yeah, and I'm hoping you'll do something stupid."

"Like you did when you shot Dan Clay's campaign manager in front of witnesses?"

Heather ground her molars as Boyd issued a sadistic laugh. Her first inclination was to take the pistol from the waistband of her jeans and empty it into the man. It took great effort, but she stilled her emotions.

Boyd then said, "You gotta' love our judicial system. All it took was one mistake and I'm a free man."

Steve goaded him in return. "What happened to your voice? Did you have a bad night on the cell block? I hear they have rough parties. Did your boyfriend get carried away and choke you?"

"Keep on, Smiley, and you'll have the last afternoon of your life."

Heather knew Steve was picking a fight with Bill Boyd, but she didn't like the direction the conversation was going. It was time for a distraction. "Hey!" she shouted. "We didn't come here to talk to the hired help. Take us to Leonard Spears before he jerks your chain again and tears up what's left of your voice."

Heather watched as Boyd picked up the metal-detecting wand from the edge of the table. "Put your arms out from your side."

He moved toward her as she held arms outstretched and said, "If that wand touches me, you'll be missing some teeth."

The wand passed slowly over her front, from shoes to the top of her head. "Hold the tail of your shirt out."

"Look, pervert. I didn't come here so you could examine the goods."

"Do it," shouted Boyd.

Heather picked up the front corners of the loose-fitting blouse with a busy print, which revealed a base layer of a clingy knit top.

He took more time than was necessary to look for a weapon.

Heather interrupted the examination of her assets. "You've seen enough. We have business to conduct with your boss."

"I agree," said Steve. "I know your boss doesn't like to be kept waiting. We don't want you to have to sit in a corner with a dunce hat on."

Heather turned around, giving him a quick peek at the backside before dropping the blouse over her tank top.

A voice came over a speaker on the ceiling. "What's the holdup? Wand them and bring them to me."

The ex-con ran the wand over Heather's backside, gave Steve a quick once-over, and said, "Let's go. Up the stairs and into the first office. You go first, McBlythe. Try anything cute, and they'll plant Smiley next to his wife."

He turned and his jacket came open. Heather caught a glimpse of what looked like a Colt 1911 in a shoulder holster. She considered the stopping power of Boyd's .45 versus the .32 in the back of her pants and didn't like the odds. She hoped Steve's commitment to talking instead of shooting would allow everyone to leave under their own power and not in a body bag.

Accompanied by the giant schnauzer, the three walked up the stairs. With her blouse and tank top covering her waistband, she was sure the gun couldn't be seen. So far, so good.

The metal stairs emptied onto a solid walkway that led to three doors with glass fronts overlooking the warehouse. The first door was already open.

Heather didn't need to be told to go in. She recognized Leonard Spears from the pictures in the background files they'd compiled. He stood and extended his hand. She didn't shake it.

Steve followed her in, as did Bill Boyd, who stood on his boss's right side, a step back, but close enough to watch them both and react if necessary. This put Steve in front of a chair facing the middle of the desk. Heather and her chair were on Steve's right, farthest from the door. Le Roi sat by Steve's left side, with ears up, on full alert, his eyes focused on Boyd.

Spears began by saying, "Please have a seat. I hate to look up at people while I'm conducting business."

Steve and Heather settled into their seats, leaving only Boyd standing.

Spears took a long look at Le Roi. "What a magnificent dog. I've never seen a giant schnauzer used as a service dog to the blind."

Steve gave Le Roi a pat on the head. "He's the extra-large version and one heck of a guard dog. It's people like Bill Boyd that make me thankful for him. Did you know Bill tried to poison him a few days ago with antifreeze?"

Leonard's face clouded over, and he turned to look up at his bodyguard. "Is that true, Bill?"

"So what? It's just a dog. Smiley deserves more than that for what he did to me."

"He only did what he should have done, and I don't take kindly to you harming anyone or anything without me knowing about it first. Is that clear?"

"Yeah, but—"

Spears cut him off. "I didn't ask for an explanation. I asked if you were clear about what I said."

"Yeah, sure. I understand."

Heather took note that the tone of his voice meant Boyd understood the words, but he'd look for ways to not comply with them.

Her mind worked to process the level of threat Boyd posed to her and Steve. Bucky Franklin would try to destroy their property, but Bill Boyd was a different kind of evil. He'd kill without remorse and had to be stopped.

# Chapter Twenty-Four

Spears cleared his throat. "Bill, Mr. Smiley came here under a flag of truce, even after you tried to kill his dog. That shows true character." He paused. "I'm most displeased with your actions, but we'll deal with that matter later."

He let out a deep sigh and shifted his gaze. "Mr. Smiley, you asked for this meeting, but gave me few details other than you believed my life and business might be in danger. What makes you think that?"

Steve folded his hands on his lap. "Ms. McBlythe and I are investigating the death of Dan Clay. As you might guess, the police believe you could be responsible for it." He modified his last statement. "Not just could be, but that you sanctioned his murder."

"That doesn't surprise me."

"Stewart Clay also believes you intend to kill him." Steve once again corrected words. "Pardon me. I'm a little out of practice. I should have said that they find it more believable that the man standing to your right killed Dan Clay and intends to kill Stewart Clay."

"That's a serious accusation."

"True. Mr. Clay has overplayed his hand without sufficient proof, but he has other ways of harming you."

Spears folded his hands on his desk. "How so?"

"He's putting pressure on every politician and top law enforcement official in the state. It's only a matter of time before the coroner stops slow-walking his findings and declares the death a homicide. When that happens, you can expect visits from various law enforcement agencies, county and state inspectors, and perhaps a federal agency or two. Stewart Clay has the political pull to make it happen."

Spears moved his right hand to his face and rubbed some whisker stubble. "I know you've heard this a thousand times in your career as a detective, but I had nothing to do with Dan Clay's death."

Heather joined the conversation. "It's common knowledge that you hated Dan. The police still believe you ordered the hit that resulted in the death of his campaign manager." She held up an index finger. "One more thing to consider. You didn't know Mr. Boyd tried to kill our animals. Did he also kill Dan Clay without your knowledge?"

Boyd glared at her. "You're not pinning that on me."

"That remains to be seen," said Steve. "Can you prove where you were on the night of his murder?"

"Uh..."

Heather jumped in next. "It would be so much easier if you confessed and took your punishment like a man."

Steve added, "That is, if you still claim to be a man."

Blood flowed upward into Boyd's face, changing its color to something between pink and red. "I know how cops and the courts work. They can't convict me without proof, and even if they do, I can beat the rap on appeal."

"Perhaps," said Heather. "But every cop and prosecutor

knows you're guilty of killing Dan Clay's campaign manager. It's only natural that they suspect you of killing Stewart Clay's son."

Leonard leaned forward. "You've made your point about Bill being more of a liability than an asset. Here's what I don't understand. Why are you telling me this?"

Steve took over. "I don't think I've told you anything yet that you don't already know except this..." He allowed the words to dangle in the air. "The trigger-happy oaf standing next to you is dumb enough to start a war with Stewart Clay. Heather and I have been to the Clay's home in River Oaks. It's more like a fortress than you've made this place. They have the advantage over you because the police are on their side."

"Cops don't scare me," said Boyd.

"That's because you're stupid," said Steve. "You couldn't even kill my dog."

Heather saw the look in Boyd's eyes, slipped her right hand to the small of her back, and grasped the small pistol.

Steve kept goading Boyd. "Did you hear me, brainless? I sent you to prison once, and I'll do it again. This time for trying to kill my dog."

Boyd's body shook with fury. "I'm not going back, but you'll need to get a new dog." His hand reached for his pistol. Heather had hers out with one smooth motion. She hollered, "Drop it!"

Shocked at the sight of the pistol pointing at him, Boyd froze, his own gun half-drawn from his jacket. Before she could give him another command, he came to his senses and raised his gun. With the business end of the .45 pointed at her chest and his finger on the hammer, Le Roi launched himself toward the man. His jaws clamped down on Boyd's arm with a sickening crunch. The pistol clattered onto the floor as Boyd screamed in pain. Le Roi shook the arm like it was a ragdoll until Steve told him to stop and heel.

The entire attack took only a few seconds. Heather retrieved the large pistol and carried it back to her chair. She then wiped the ceramic one clean. Her next move was to place both pistols on Spears's desk.

Steve asked. "Is everything all right?"

"I'm fine," said Heather. "I didn't like your plan until Boyd confessed to poisoning Max."

"Who's Max?" asked Spears.

"My cat," said Heather. "He drank some of the antifreeze and almost died."

Steve directed a smile to Spears. "I trained Le Roi to not drink antifreeze, but training cats is a different story. Your man Bill poisoned Heather's cat, and she doesn't tolerate anyone harming Max."

Heather added, "Or anyone that I consider family or a close friend."

Boyd remained on the floor, writhing in pain and making quite a racket. Steve asked, "Would you mind sending someone up to remove your now worthless intimidator? We still have things to discuss with you."

Spears took the desk phone's receiver from its cradle and punched a button. He gave instructions for Butch to come to his office without delay.

The man arrived but Spears didn't give him time to say anything. "Put the rifle in the corner and take Boyd downstairs. Don't let him leave. Wrap his arm in a towel, but that's all. Lock him in the janitor's closet and don't let him near a gun."

The door closed behind the men, and Steve turned to Heather. "How much time do we have?"

"Twenty-two minutes."

"Mr. Spears," said Steve. "Bill is unstable. You saw it with your own eyes. We also proved that he's incompetent and a liability to your enterprises. The police will be here in about twenty-one minutes if they don't hear from us. That gives enough time for us to finish our business and for you to decide what you're going to do with Bill Boyd."

Steve added, "An extra-large giant schnauzer has a biting strength of over five hundred pounds per square inch. His arm will never be the same. It's your decision what to do with Bill. Handing him over to the police, along with that very illegal gun, is one option."

Spears interlaced his fingers and rested his hands on his desk. "What else do we have to discuss?"

"Like we said earlier, we're hired to find the person or persons responsible for Dan Clay's death. Right now, we have multiple suspects. You're still at the top of the list."

"For you two or the police?"

"Don't include me," said Heather. "The attempt on my cat's life clouds my judgment. Steve and I don't always agree until we find more evidence, or someone confesses."

Spears leaned back and unclenched his hands. "You won't find any evidence that links me to Dan Clay's murder."

"That may be true, but your reputation with the police is not what I'd call squeaky-clean."

Spears narrowed his eyes. "Speak in plain English. I'm a simple man who makes his living dealing with simple people."

Steve took over. "Were you in any way involved in the murder of Dan Clay?"

"No."

"Was Bill Boyd or anyone else who works for you involved in the murder of Dan Clay?"

"Not to my knowledge."

"Were you in any way involved in the attempted murder of Dan Clay that resulted in Bill Boyd shooting the wrong man?"

"I'll not answer that."

"You just did."

Heather and Steve rose at the same time.

Steve ended the meeting with a few parting words. "My advice to you is not to go after Stewart Clay. It's a war you can't win."

# Chapter Twenty-Five

Heather slid into the front passenger seat while Steve's seatbelt made its distinctive click, assuring her he was ready for the trip home. Rasheed soon joined them, and she heard Le Roi and Princess pacing beyond the back seat.

Steve said, "Princess must smell Bill Boyd's blood. Do you think she knows she missed out on the action?"

"What action?" asked Rasheed.

Heather blew out a breath of what seemed like dirty air. "Let's get out of this depressing dump. If you two don't mind, I need to spend some time recalibrating."

That was all it took for Steve and Rasheed to remain quiet. Heather closed her eyes and used meditation techniques until the sound of jet engines flying overhead brought her out of a self-imposed mental exile. "We must be passing the airport." She opened her eyes and confirmed their location.

Rasheed shot her a quick glance. "Am I to assume that your meeting was not a success?"

"It all depends how you measure success," said Steve. "We

accomplished much but took some moral shortcuts to get to our destination."

"Exactly," said Heather. "We exacted revenge on the man who almost killed Max. He was trying to kill Steve for arresting him many years ago."

Steve took his turn. "It occurred to me yesterday that it wasn't Bucky who put out the bowl of antifreeze."

"How did you determine that?"

"Le Roi and Princess are both trained to react violently to Bucky's scent. That didn't happen when we found Max. It took me a while to realize it, but when I did, I knew it had to be someone else with a grudge against me. Heather helped me talk it through last night and she came up with Bill Boyd as the primary suspect. We plotted to spring a trap on Boyd. It worked when Le Roi caught his scent when we entered the warehouse. He literally vibrated and stayed on high alert until he saved our lives."

Heather added, "We goaded Boyd until he flew into a blind rage and tried to pull a pistol on us. Le Roi sprang into action. The former enforcer's right arm is a dangling mess."

The interior of the car quieted, and they once more traveled in silence for several miles. Rasheed broke the silence by saying, "If either or both of you are experiencing guilt over the man's injuries, that's perfectly normal."

"Keep talking," said Steve. "I could use some counseling, or at least some sage advice."

A long pause preceded Rasheed's words. "Revenge is like a beautiful pie made with sour apples and salt instead of sugar."

Heather looked out the window. "I'm tasting it now."

Steve responded with, "Sometimes those are the only ingredients we're given to cook with."

"Very true, my friends. That's when you thank God for salt,

apples, and deliverance from harm. Your time for a better tasting pie will come again."

"It can't come soon enough," said Heather. "Solving murders rejuvenates my mind, but this one is taxing my ethics."

Steve countered with, "One or two more unpleasant interviews and we should be able to bring this case in for a landing."

Heather asked, "Will it be a crash landing or a smooth one?"

Rasheed answered for Steve. "It is said that any landing you walk away from is good enough."

Steve added a postscript. "Someone's going to walk away wearing handcuffs. I don't know who yet, but someone will."

Rasheed had one more suggestion. "Napoleon said that an army marches on its stomach. I suggest we fill ours."

"Great idea," said Steve. "I already know what I want for dessert. A big slice of apple pie made the way I like it. Plenty of sugar and a scoop of vanilla ice cream on top."

Heather couldn't help but smile. "For once, I agree with your prescription for treating guilt. Let's splurge."

———

FOLLOWING the stop at a local cafe, the trio made their way home, where the dogs couldn't wait to roam the vast area inside the fence, all the way to the water's edge. Steve made it to his recliner and collapsed in what appeared to be a pie and ice cream-induced coma.

Heather left him there and went to her home's office. She glanced at the time and placed a call. Jack answered with his standard greeting when he was in his office alone. "Hello, beautiful."

"Hello, handsome. Are you leaned back in your chair with your boots on the desk?"

"You know me too well. It's been a full day and I'm enjoying a few minutes thinking of you."

"More likely, you're thinking about fishing."

"That too, but I'm daydreaming of pulling my boat up to your lot and dropping off fish for you to clean and cook for supper."

Heather rolled her eyes. "You sure know how to sweet talk a girl."

"How was your trip to Houston?"

Heather had known this question was coming but delayed, making sure she had her emotions under control. "The trip went the way Steve and I planned it. We went to a rusty warehouse in the sketchiest part of town, came close to getting shot, Le Roi attacked a bad guy and mauled his arm, then we stopped on the way home and I had an enormous slice of apple pie and ice cream. You know, a normal day."

Jack chuckled. "You had me going until you said you had an enormous piece of pie and ice cream."

She smiled at the thought of him not believing her. If he ever learned the truth, she could honestly say she didn't lie to him.

"By the way," said Jack. "I had a brilliant attorney apply for a job today. Her name is Junani Hasan. Ring a bell?"

Heather gasped. "Yeah. It rings several bells. I was going to call her to see if she's still interested in coming to work for me after what happened last night."

"Am I allowed to ask what happened?"

"You just did, and it was a date with Rasheed. He tried too hard to impress her and the perfect romantic dinner turned into a five-alarm dumpster fire."

"That explains her red eyes. She must have soaked her pillow with tears."

"That's a good sign," said Heather. "Women rarely cry like

that if they don't care about the guy. How did she come across in the interview?"

"Not great."

"Good. You can't have her."

A hint of mischief came into Jack's voice. "What would you say if I told you I hired her?"

"I'd say you're not a very convincing liar."

The loud squeak from Jack's chair meant he'd taken his boots off the desk, a sure sign the conversation was ending. "What's the chance of us getting together this weekend?"

"Fishing?"

"Of course."

"Only if Steve and I finish the case in the next two days and it's a catch and release fishing trip."

"It's a deal," said Jack. "Got to go. It's past five and I hate to work overtime."

The call ended with the normal words of parting. Heather placed her cell phone on her desk, and her thoughts turned to Claire Strobel. She'd made an appointment with the environmentalist to come to her office the following afternoon. Steve had taken in the information but seemed to dismiss it. He apparently didn't want to talk about Claire until after they'd spoken with Leonard Spears and done something about Bill Boyd. That unsavory task was now complete, and it was time to move on to the next suspect.

She yawned, something she rarely did this time of day. Perhaps a brief nap was what she needed to refresh her mind and body. She and Steve would plan the meeting later that night or the following morning.

A physical and emotional crash followed the sugar rush. She barely made it into bed before Max settled into the crook of her body. She awakened when Princess shot from her bed and nudged the bedroom door open with her nose.

Heather looked at the time on her phone, then slipped out of bed and padded her way to the kitchen where Steve sat on a barstool. Instead of a normal greeting, he began the day with a question. "Did you sleep in that?"

She looked down at her mostly bare legs and a long T-shirt. "I guess I did. I changed out of what I wore to Houston after I called Jack. That's the last thing I remember besides getting into bed. I can't believe I slept all night."

She shook her head to rid the cobwebs from her mind. "Wait. How do you know what I have on? Did you recover your sight during the night?"

Steve chuckled. "Unfortunately not. It was an educated guess. I figured between the emotional high of yesterday's encounter and the sugar rush, you might lie down in the clothes you had on and crash out."

"You never stop, do you?" She shook her head. "Aided by a lavender scented sleep mask and a loop playing the sounds of waves lapping to shore, my nap turned into a deep, dreamless sleep."

"You should be rested enough to run a marathon. Is there any chance you could operate that new spaceship you call a coffee maker? I felt it and gave up trying to figure it out."

Heather moved toward the machine that would make most coffee shops swoon with envy and changed the subject. "Have you been outside this morning?"

"Warm and windy. I imagine the lake is kicking up. Not a great day for being on the water, which is fine. We need to discuss how you're going to handle today's meeting with Claire Strobel."

She stopped packing coffee into the machine's portafilter and looked at Steve. "Why didn't you include yourself in the interview with Claire?"

"Because you're going to do it without me. I'll be listening from the soundproof recording room."

"I thought we were going to come up with a plan together."

A mischievous grin pulled up one corner of his mouth. "You snooze, you lose. I was ready to talk last night, but you went to a tropical island." He kept talking. "Are you making me an espresso?"

"I was, now I'm not so sure. I have some ideas of my own about how we'd conduct the interview."

"You can ask whatever you want, as long as you include my questions and I'm not in the room with you when you ask them."

"Why not? Give me one good reason you shouldn't be with me to interview her."

Steve rubbed his chin and said, "She hates men. Didn't you read or listen to her speeches? Claire blames men for ninety-nine percent of everything that's detrimental to the environment. It would be one hundred percent if it weren't for the fashion and cosmetics industries." He took a breath. "At least that's what she says in public."

Heather went back to the espresso machine. She spoke to herself more than she did to Steve. "I should have caught that aspect of her personality."

Steve spoke with a purposefully pretentious tone to his words. "I'll cut you some slack this time. Max's near-death experience had you preoccupied. Now that he's safe, we've taken our pound of flesh from his attacker, and you've caught up on your sleep, we can move forward with solving this case."

"Are we close?"

"We'll know for sure after today's interview. Take your laptop to the back porch. I wrote you a long email. Add your ideas to what I want you to ask Claire. It should be an interesting interview."

# Chapter Twenty-Six

Heather's meeting on her back porch with Steve lasted until a few minutes before ten. The sun had crept over the roof of her home and bore down on them. A large umbrella provided shade, but the wind had calmed and they both dabbed sweat away.

They agreed to meet in an hour and have Rasheed drive them to work. The chauffeur's arrival reminded Heather that she needed to do something about getting a commitment from Junani to accept or reject her job offer. Romance or not, she was more than qualified, and her area of specialty fit well with the direction the company needed to go. Today, however, would not be the day Heather made the offer. She wouldn't allow her mind to be distracted with business when Steve believed they were so close to solving the case and delivering it to Leo with a pretty red bow.

As expected, Rasheed arrived with a down-turned smile. His emotions had still not recovered from the disastrous supper date. To his credit, he tried to act normally. Steve helped by distracting him on the drive to the office with a wild story about another armadillo. It seems a friend of his in high school captured the creature and placed it in the car of a classmate who'd been threatening him. Unbeknownst to his friend, the car needed repair. A week in August passed without the car being opened. Steve went into detail about the attempts to clean the car, all to no avail. The stench had permeated everything but metal.

Rasheed responded to the story with a trio of original parables, each better than the one before it. In an odd turn of events, her driver arrived at the office in a much better mood.

Heather didn't know if there was an ounce of truth in Steve's tale or if he made it up to help Rasheed. True or not, it worked to pull him out of the doldrums.

Steve decided he would spend the next two hours writing his short story. Heather had no objection to this, as he'd already conveyed in writing and orally what he wanted her to say. They'd also discussed her ideas and established a plan that pleased them both.

She remained on the elevator with Princess as Steve, Rasheed, and Le Roi exited at the third floor. Pam, her personal assistant, waited for her arrival in the outer office. Once inside the inner sanctum, Heather asked, "Any disasters I need to know about?"

"Nothing that can't wait."

She pulled her laptop from her satchel and placed it on her desk but didn't open it. "I want to call my father and then you can tell me about the mini disasters. Give me ten minutes."

Pam gave her a knowing look. "You and Steve must be close to the end. You're wanting to know about work. That only happens when you're within a day or two."

Heather lifted her shoulders and let them fall. "I read Steve for subtle clues that tell me he's close. Then, you do the same to me. All I can say is, don't look for me to be in tomorrow."

Pam changed the subject. "I tested the audio and video in the interview room. Everything's ready."

"Thank you. Steve will be in the sound room, listening with Le Roi."

"Are any police coming?"

"Not this time, but our guest is a female with a history of multiple arrests. I'll keep Princess with me, just in case she's offended by some of my questions."

"Should I have building security in the room with Steve?"

Heather shook her head. "I saw what Le Roi can do to a man with a gun yesterday. I have a newfound level of respect for trained police dogs."

Pam's eyes widened before she slammed her eyelids shut and held up a hand. "Don't tell me anymore. The thought of you and Steve in danger will ruin my sleep for a week."

The personal assistant made for the door. "I'm going to pop a Xanax and be back in fifteen minutes. Enjoy your talk with your father."

The conversation with her father only lasted eight minutes, but it was long enough for him to guess the case was nearing an end. They each spoke with staccato sentences that conveyed facts. Paternal concern laced his words toward the end. "On a scale of one to ten, how would you rate the danger you're in with today's interview?"

"Less than two," said Heather.

"And yesterday's?"

"Uh... em... a little higher."

"How high? Give me a number."

"On a scale of one to ten, I'd rate it a solid nine."

Her father let out a rush of air. "That's too high. You wouldn't make a business deal with a ninety percent chance of failure. Promise me you won't go over fifty percent with your next case."

"I'll be as careful as I can and still achieve positive results. You taught me that with high risks come big rewards." She turned around in her chair and looked out the window. "Princess will be with me today and the interview will take place in my building. The woman I'm interviewing uses words for weapons, not firearms."

"It's not today's interview that concerns me. It's all the ones in the future."

"Dad," said Heather in a softer tone. "Let's not borrow trouble from the future. Pam is coming back in a few minutes with a couple of business problems for me to deal with."

"Speaking of," said her father. "I have one more employee coming in that I need to fire this afternoon."

"Was he selling secrets?"

"She, and yes, she was."

"How did you catch her?"

"I followed the money. It led straight to her, and to the others I'd already let go."

Heather ended the call, but her father's advice of following the money struck a chord.

Pam knocked and entered her office. The two minor disasters turned out to be a late payment by bookkeeping to the IRS and a lawsuit from a contractor demanding additional money for a road accident while making a delivery to her lake project.

Heather took the last problem first. "I'm familiar with the accident claim and it's frivolous. There's no rush to respond to it. When I come back to work, set up a meeting between me, the head of legal, and the attorney handling the case. As for the late payment, I want to know why it's late. Get me a written explanation from the person responsible. If that person recently quit, I bet they did some creative accounting and took a bonus with them. Tell legal to hire a forensic accountant if necessary. People rarely forget to pay the IRS."

Pam didn't need to write the instructions. She looked at Heather. "Always follow the money. Right?"

"That's the path to the problem most of the time."

"If that's the path, what's the root problem?"

"Greed, love, or love's cousin, lust."

Pam turned to leave. "I'll run down the hall and tell legal to get on it right away."

The click of the door closing made Heather think of a dimmer switch. The words of her father concerning money, and her conversation with Pam about motives, turned the switch a little, but not enough to give her full illumination. She wondered if Steve, even though he was blind, had already turned his internal dimmer switch full blast and knew the identity of Dan Clay's killer.

She spent an indeterminate amount of time trying to turn up the dimmer, but an identity eluded her. Steve entered and said, "Claire should be here soon. Le Roi and I are going to the soundproof room and wait. Pam and Rasheed wanted to join me. Any objections?"

"None. They can tell you what they're seeing."

# Chapter Twenty-Seven

Heather instructed Pam to meet Claire at the elevator and escort her to the interview room. It was a last-minute decision, but one that made more sense than having Claire come to her office, only for them to leave and travel down the hallway.

Claire entered the room with suspicion painted on her face like theatrical makeup. Pam exited as quickly as she entered, leaving Heather to rise from a wingback chair and greet her guest. "Hello, Ms. Strobel. Thank you for traveling to talk to me."

Her guest spied the one-way glass and pointed. "What's with the spy-glass?"

Heather flipped the question away with her hand and walked toward what looked like a mirror. "This is where we interview prospective employees and handle personnel problems. There's a camera on the other side. Department heads do most of the hiring and firing, but sometimes I want to be the tiebreaker on a close call. The recordings allow me to keep up with my busy schedule and make decisions at my convenience."

Heather gave her head a slight tilt. "If the glass bothers you, I can close the curtains."

"I'll do it," said Claire with bravado.

Heather stood back as Claire examined the thick curtains and looked even closer at her reflection in the glass. She then pulled the cord that closed the fabric and overlapped the glass edges on all four sides.

Heather took the time to give Claire a closer look. She'd dressed much the same as the day they met at Galveston's John Sealy Hospital. Heather would describe the loose-fitting peasant dress as an attempt to look bohemian. A headscarf fashioned from a blue bandanna and brown Huarache sandals completed the late 1960's look. The only thing missing was square-lensed, wire-framed glasses.

Claire then took a lap around the room, gazing at anything that caught her eye.

"If you're looking for a camera, they're stored in another room. If you want, I can record our conversation and send it to you."

"No," snapped Claire. "I don't know what you're up to, but I don't trust you."

"Yet, you came anyway. Why?"

"It's simple. You said you were interested in protecting the environment. I can tell you how."

"And remain profitable?"

"And become even more profitable."

Heather hoped her expression showed doubt. "That's a big claim. Can you back it up?"

Claire settled into a club chair that had her facing a camera hidden in an air conditioning duct. Her scowl morphed into an overconfident smile. "I can help you in ways that will astound you, but I may not want to. We in the movement are very restrictive in who we allow to participate in our enterprises."

Heather scrunched her eyebrows together. "Are you saying I need to qualify? You can find my holdings on my website, along with a profit-and-loss statement. Surely you know my company's net worth and my investments, or you wouldn't have come. What else do you need?"

Claire leaned forward. "I deal with companies like yours every day. You say you want to help the environment, but what you really want is more."

"More what?" asked Heather.

"More money. What else is there?"

Heather didn't respond, so Claire kept talking. "I know the people who can boost your profits by ten to fifty percent. I can either be your best friend or your worst enemy."

Heather blanched. "I have no need for any additional enemies."

Claire settled back in her chair. "Good. Now we're clear on where we stand."

"Not exactly," said Heather. "Up to now, all we've discussed is me and my company. It shouldn't surprise you I've done some research and know you're backed by powerful people and organizations."

"More powerful than you can imagine."

"I'd prefer not to have them as enemies."

Heather named off a handful of domestic organizations with a reputation for using boycotts, protests, and legal measures to disrupt companies.

Claire laughed. "You have international businesses, too. We're especially effective outside the US."

Heather took a breath and scooted to the edge of her seat. "Becoming a successful businesswoman wasn't easy and I don't react well to bullies like you, so you can cut the bad-girl act."

Claire stiffened. "It's no act. The people I work for can break you."

Heather shrugged. "Perhaps. Perhaps not. I'm also a pragmatist. That means I look at things from a cost-benefit point of view. Up to now, we've danced around some very important issues. First, what must I do to keep the people you work for from trying to destroy me? In short, what's it going to cost me?"

"That's not the right question. You should ask how much extra you'll make from the good press you'll receive when you get a green seal on all your businesses."

"Cut to the chase," said Heather. "How much do you charge for the green seal?"

"Not that much for you, because your businesses are already eighty-two percent environmentally friendly. The green certifications for the remaining products should pay for themselves three times over on the remaining eighteen percent."

"How much?" demanded Heather.

Claire gave a lecherous smile. "Only 2 percent of company profits."

Heather had what she needed to complete one third of Steve's plan. The door opened and in came Rasheed with Princess.

Claire climbed into her chair and screamed. "Get that dog out of here."

Princess ran to Heather's side, turned to face Claire, exposed her teeth and growled.

"Take it away. Take it away," shouted Claire.

Heather said, "Look at her vest. She's a therapy dog. She wouldn't hurt anyone unless they tried to hurt me. All you need to do is calm yourself and sit down. Not only do you look silly, your behavior is making her think you're a threat."

"I'm not coming down until that dog's gone."

"I have a better idea. You tell me everything you know about Dan Clay and I'll hold the dog back."

"Who's Dan Clay?"

"Don't play like you don't know him. You've been trying to extort money from his father for years."

Claire's eyes searched the room for an answer. She finally hit on it. "Dan Clay? Isn't he the son of Stewart Clay, of Clay Oil?"

Revelation came slowly, but it finally came. "Wait a minute. Dan Clay died recently. Some sort of drowning accident."

"Not an accident," said Heather. "Someone murdered him, and you're going to tell me all you know about Dan."

Steve's voice came from the hallway. "That's all, Heather."

This wasn't the way they'd planned to end the meeting. She thought this was only the prelude to the grilling Claire would receive.

Heather didn't know why he'd stopped her, and she wasn't going home until she did.

Rasheed approached her, and she handed him Princess's leash and told her dog to go with the chauffeur.

Confusion and frustration competed in Heather's mind. She brought her emotions under partial control and looked up at Claire. "For heaven's sake, come down from that chair. You look ridiculous. Almost as ridiculous as you did when you tried to extort money from me. Now, get out of my building before I have what's left of you taken to the hospital. My dog looks hungry."

Claire didn't need the instruction repeated.

Heather took a few extra minutes of silence before returning to her office. Did Steve have a legitimate reason for ending her interview with Claire so abruptly? Legitimate or not, she didn't appreciate the way he'd handled it.

She stood, brushed a wrinkle out of her skirt, and told herself to get the facts before tearing into him with a full-throated broadside.

It took effort not to stomp down the hall like she had as a teen when she didn't get her way. Her mother's raised right eyebrow signaled the warning. If she added a raised chin, that meant consequences. Her mother only gave one warning. Next came the outstretched hand to receive Heather's lifeline to the outside world—her cell phone.

As she walked, she wondered what she could do to Steve that would be equivalent to her mother's discipline. Nothing came to mind. How do you punish a grown man who's also blind? Facial expressions meant nothing to him. Only the tone of her voice and the words themselves. That being the case, she had some choice ones ready to share.

She passed Rasheed in the hallway. "Mr. Steve told me to go to my office and carry on with my normal duties. Princess is waiting for you in your office, as is Steve."

She nodded a thank you, not trusting her words.

The door to her office closed harder than she intended, but she gave no apology.

She walked past his desk, but turned around when she heard him say, "Have a seat where you can hear."

He activated the speaker on his phone after telling it to call Stewart Clay. It rang four times before a tired voice said, "Mr. Smiley. I'm glad you called. I need a progress report."

"Heather and I will be at your home tomorrow morning, as will some police officers and special guests."

"Will Leonard Spears be one of them?"

"Yes."

"Good. I appreciate you allowing me to see the cops slap handcuffs on him."

"Tell Fred Lawrence there will be seven sitting. I doubt if

Fred or the cops will want to sit. Also, Heather and I are bringing our dogs. The great room would probably be best."

"What time?"

"Eleven in the morning. Heather will call Fred and give him the names of everyone who needs to attend the meeting. It's imperative that everyone is there, and that we start on time."

"I'll do my part."

"And Heather and I will do ours."

The call ended and Steve spoke before she could. "Leo called me while you were having fun with Claire."

He rapped his fingers on his desk. "By the way. Great job of getting Claire to admit to extortion. Leo will detain her tomorrow morning and bring her to the meeting at Stewart's home. You'll need to send Leo a copy of the interview. He'll want the original, too, but that can wait until tomorrow."

Steve sucked in a quick breath. "The coroner finally ruled Dan Clay's death as a homicide. Leo's also taking care of having some sort of state police there to arrest the killers."

Heather bolted out of her chair and placed her hands firmly on the edge of Steve's desk. "If you don't slow down and tell me what's going on, I'll replace all the sugar in your house with artificial sweeteners."

"You wouldn't dare."

"Little packets of pink and blue." She watched him make a face that looked like a cartoon character spitting out something putrid.

"You win," said Steve. "I'll slow down. First, I know who killed Dan."

"Do you also know why, and do you have proof?"

"Yes, and almost... at least I have enough proof to get them to confess."

Steve then asked, "Do you know if Bella's busy tomorrow?"

"I can ask," she said tersely.

"Good. I'll tell you all the details then you can decide if we should include her."

Heather sat back down and crossed her legs. "I won't be able to decide if you don't start talking."

# Chapter Twenty-Eight

Moisture-laden clouds raced to the northwest as Rasheed guided Heather's car south. Their destination was the home of Stewart and Lisa Clay in the River Oaks section of Houston. The first half of the trip had been quiet, with anticipation of the day's events building.

Nervous energy finally got the best of Heather and she turned as far as she could and spoke over her left shoulder to Steve. "What if your plan for a quick confession doesn't pan out?"

"Then the police will take what we give them and try to finish what we started. It will mean more work for them, but at least we've ruled out some people."

He gave a mirthless chuckle. "We'll also have an unhappy client. It's a good thing we aren't counting on making a living from this private detective gig. The cases are too far apart, and we usually forget to charge."

Rasheed chimed in. "The man who weaves only one day a week makes short blankets."

"And has cold feet," added Steve.

Heather had just swallowed a sip of coffee when the mental image hit her. A second or two earlier, and she would have sprayed the warm liquid on the dashboard.

A wide smile parted Rasheed's lips. "We almost had a repeat of Steve's date with the woman he married. I should make a proverb addressing the perils of eating and drinking in a vehicle."

The levity broke the anxiety brought on by Heather's unhealthy fear of failure. She leaned back in her seat and began a silent recitation of things she was thankful for. This brought her into a peaceful state of mind, which included a feeling of confidence. Steve might keep things from her too long for her liking, but he'd told her every aspect of his plan and sought her input to make it better. Who could ask for a better business partner, especially when the business was solving murders?

The gate to the Clay mansion swung open. A few scattered drops of rain greeted them, as did Fred Lawrence, dressed in what looked like the same dark suit, white shirt, and tie. He waited until they were in the entry before saying, "I don't like this."

Steve handled the question. "What don't you like?"

"Bringing Leonard Spears here. I don't trust him."

"He's coming alone. His lead bodyguard, Bill Boyd, had an unfortunate encounter with a big black dog yesterday."

"Boyd's a hot head. It serves him right."

Heather spoke. "I witnessed the encounter, and it upset me severely. I have to insist my dog accompanies me."

Fred Lawrence gave the dog a suspicious gaze. "The vest says the shepherd is a service dog. Is that true?"

"She's fully trained and dual certified as a therapy and police dog."

"Mine, too," said Steve. "Both of them can sense trouble before it happens. They're also trained to detect plastic and ceramic ghost guns, not to mention regular firearms. Heather will make sure Leonard Spears and all the other guests aren't armed." He added a postscript. "All but the police who are coming."

Heather turned to Steve. "Rasheed will get you and Le Roi settled in the great room. I'll stay here with Fred and let Princess give everyone a good sniff."

Leo and his female partner were the next to arrive. Claire Strobel wore handcuffs as an accessory to her bohemian outfit. Otherwise, she looked the same as she had yesterday in the interview room.

Claire stared daggers at Heather, but a deep growl from Princess stilled the embezzler's voice. Leo and his partner hustled her down the hallway leading to the great room as Leo quipped, "I've got to get me a dog like Princess. One growl and this woman shut her yapping."

The buzzer sounded and Fred moved to a small screen mounted on the wall. A metallic voice said, "It's Leonard Spears."

Fred pushed a button. "Are you alone?"

"Yeah. That's the way Ms. McBlythe told me to come."

"Are you armed?"

"There's a pistol under the seat, but nothing on me."

"Come through."

Fred pushed the button beside the one that operated the camera and microphone. He then took out a radio from his jacket pocket and keyed the microphone. "Spears is coming through the front gate. If any other vehicles try to follow him, take them out."

Heather breathed a sigh of relief when the gate shut behind Spears's car. She and Princess went to the front porch. Two men dressed as gardeners appeared from behind trees with rifles trained on the approaching car.

Heather issued a warning. "Fred, if they shoot, you'll go to prison."

"They won't fire unless he comes out with a gun in his hand."

The car came to a stop as Heather and Princess approached it, even though Fred told her not to.

The door came open and Heather stationed herself between Fred and Spears. "Don't make any quick moves. Come out with your hands up. There are two rifles pointed at you, and the guy behind me wants an excuse to see if his pistol still works."

Spears complied, and Heather gave the next command. "Relax and don't make any sudden moves. My dog is going to walk around you. If you're carrying a gun, you'll experience what Boyd did."

"The only weapon is under the seat. I work in a rough part of town."

"Search," said Heather in a firm voice. Princess moved like a dart to sniff from chest to shoes as she made a quick lap around Spears.

"He's clean," announced Heather.

"Have the dog check the car."

Heather kicked the door shut. "Tell your men to check it and put the pistol back when they're finished. We're getting wet and it's about to pour."

Heather gave Princess her reward of a good rub on her head and rib cage. She walked beside Spears with Princess between them and Fred following behind.

Once inside, Fred issued a final warning to Spears. "I'll be standing directly behind you. I can get this nine mil out and have three slugs in you before you can stand."

Heather stopped and turned to stare at Fred. "You and my driver both sound like cheap gangsters. Give it a break, will you? I'll have to listen to him all the way home if you get trigger-happy."

Heather and Princess turned and walked on. They made it into the great room where she and her dog sat next to Steve and Le Roi, with a giant fireplace behind them.

The patriarch, Stewart Clay, sat in front of the hidden door leading to his private office. His much younger wife, Lisa, sat next to her husband. Leonard Spears chose a chair opposite Stewart, as far away as he could get. Fred Lawrence, the bodyguard, stood behind him.

Directly opposite Steve sat Claire Strobel with Leo's partner on the same couch, an arm's length apart. Leo stood behind them with a clear view of everyone in the room, just like Steve had taught him.

The first clap of thunder sounded. It was like nature was giving the signal to begin. Fred Lawrence broke the tension and the silence. "Where are the others? I thought we were going to start at eleven."

A clock chimed. "Now we can start," said Steve. "The others should be along in a little while. Let's begin with Leonard Spears."

"Let's start and end with him," said Stewart Clay. "He had his man try to kill Dan when my son ran for city council. Bill Boyd succeeded after Spears bribed a judge to release him from prison."

Spears shot back. "I never ordered a hit on your son. Boyd took it upon himself to do that, and I didn't pay a dime to appeal his conviction, either. That was a story I made up because I hate to lose."

"Wait," said Fred. "If you didn't pay for the appeal, who did?"

"I have no idea. All I know is it wasn't me."

Leo nudged Claire Strobel. "Tell them or I will."

"I'm not saying anything without a lawyer." She offered a smug grin. "Besides, there's not a shred of evidence that will implicate me."

"She's right," said Steve. "Claire is what you might call a professional disruptor. She mostly works with people and organizations who espouse to be protectors of the environment, but she's branched out in recent years. Have you ever wondered where all the money comes from that clogs the courts with challenges to convictions? She could tell you, but she won't. With Bill Boyd, for example, she found a reversible error in the paperwork and notified the people who love to see guilty people go free."

Heather added, "We believe Claire examined the paperwork so carefully because the intended victim was the son of Stewart Clay and the heir apparent to Clay Oil. She's a dedicated environmentalist with a genuine hatred of fossil fuels."

"I know she hates my company," said Stewart. "Always has and most likely always will."

"You can count on that," said Claire. "What you can't count on is ever finding evidence that links me to the murder of your son's campaign manager or to your son's death. You'll also not be able to connect me to the appeal of Bill Boyd's conviction."

"I wouldn't bet on that," said Steve. "I'll ask my former partner, Detective Leo Vega, to explain that later."

"And speaking of Dan's murder," said Steve. "The coroner ruled it a homicide yesterday."

Claire shrugged the information off like it was inconsequential.

"The important thing is," said Heather, "... Leonard Spears may be guilty of many things, but killing Dan Clay isn't one of them."

Stewart wasn't ready to give up. "Indirectly he was. His

man, Bill Boyd, hooked up with that worthless protester sitting on my couch. Incidentally, oil paid for the couch you're sitting on, and petroleum products provided the power to make it."

Spears responded with, "Bill Boyd was involved in an industrial accident yesterday. He's no longer employed by my company. He mentioned moving out of state where he will seek a different career."

Heather cut him off. "Let's stick to the murder of your son, Mr. Clay." She cut her gaze to Leo. "Would you like to interview Mr. Spears any more today?"

"Not today. I know where he lives, as do many other people in law enforcement. He should expect frequent visits for some time to come."

Spears shut his eyes for three seconds before asking. "Can I leave now?"

Steve smiled. "If you do, you'll miss the best parts. We're just getting started."

Fred's radio came to life. "More cars at the front gate. Several are unmarked black SUV's."

The bodyguard took quick steps toward the hallway leading to the home's entry.

Heather waited until Fred's footsteps faded. She turned to look at Lisa. "I brought the contract for your husband to sign. It shouldn't take over five minutes for him to read and sign the paperwork and for me to notarize it."

"Good idea," said Stewart. "Let's go to my office. We'll have a drink to celebrate the company owning a lakefront home." He looked around the room. "It's five o'clock somewhere. If anyone else wants something, help yourself." He pointed. "That biggest pump jack in the corner is a bar that hides in plain sight."

# Chapter Twenty-Nine

S tewart Clay went directly to the bar in his office, added ice to a glass, and filled it a little over halfway with an amber liquid from a bottle with a blue label. He spoke over his shoulder as he added a splash of water. "Anyone else?"

"It's too early for me," said Heather as she settled into a chair and Princess lay beside her.

"I'll wait to celebrate later this afternoon," said Lisa. "You're coming with me to the lake, aren't you, dear?"

"Not today, Angel. I'll wait until the new furniture arrives and I can wake up to the smell of pines and the sounds of boats skimming across the water."

Stewart's breathing was labored by the time he slumped into his chair. He downed half the potent mixture and let out a sigh of satisfaction. "That's better. You can't imagine how many contracts I've signed with a half-empty glass of good Scotch in my hand." He laughed. "I discovered a long time ago that I made more money if my glass was half full and the other person signing had an empty glass."

"That sounds like sound business advice," said Heather. "Did that include the deals you made with my father?"

Stewart took another drink and rested the glass on a leather trivet. "The only thing I didn't like about making deals with your father was that he never touched a drop until the ink was dry and the contracts were off the table. I guess like father, like daughter?"

"I'm just a chip off the old block."

Stewart tapped the center of his desk with his index finger. "We can sit here and trade cliches or we can take care of business. You look like a woman who puts business first. Put that contract in front of me and tell me where to sign. I'll make out the check."

"Are you sure you want to pay the full amount up front?"

"My accountant is. Something about accelerated depreciation. Besides, I like to own things outright. It helps me sleep at night."

It took only a few minutes to complete the transaction and for her to paperclip the check to a short stack of papers. The notary seal was the last thing to go back into her satchel.

Stewart held up the keys for his smiling wife to take. "Here you are, hon. It's yours to decorate."

She circled the desk, hugged his neck, and delivered a kiss to his cheek. "You're the best husband in the world."

"Right now, I'm the thirstiest. Go back to our guests. I've one more thing to discuss with Heather."

Lisa almost skipped out of the room. The door closed and Stewart rose from his chair. "This drink needs refreshing. How about a glass of wine to help me celebrate?"

"I'll have what you're having but reverse the proportions of Scotch and water."

With drinks in hand, Stewart sat in the chair his wife vacated, next to Heather. He gave Heather her drink. They both sipped until Stewart broke the silence. "There's something you want to ask me. Go ahead."

"Before I do, I want to make sure." She looked down at Princess and said, "Seek."

Princess rose and went to Stewart. She started sniffing his shoes and worked her way to his chest. The slightest of cries squeaked out of the dog and she pressed her head against his chest.

Stewart patted her head. "Good girl. I wish you were around a long time ago."

Heather nursed her drink for perhaps thirty seconds before asking, "How long?"

He raised his shoulders and let them fall. "Not long enough." He took a long drink and cleared his throat. "I want to liquidate my company. There's no one I trust to take over. Tell your father. He'll know what to do. I'll make the announcement in two months. Once word gets out, it will be a free-for-all."

"What about your wife?"

"She'll get this house and nothing more. You and Steve know the reason. I can't abide a cheating woman."

Heather affirmed the news with a simple nod of her head. "And your daughter?"

"I'll let you know after today's meeting. She called me last night. I know she's coming with a woman named Bella. You and Steve arranged for her to be here. If she was involved in Dan's murder, she's not getting a penny."

Heather went to the bar and put her glass in the sink. "Everyone should be in the great room by now. If you'd like, Princess can stay with you. It helps to pet her."

"I'd like that."

Heather spoke to Princess. "Show love."

Stewart made one last stop at the minibar and returned to his chair. "Something tells me I'm going to need this."

Heather led the way back into the great room that had filled with several more stern-faced law enforcement officers. One badge, in particular, caught her eye. It was a small silver badge pinned to a white dress shirt. Leo had included a Texas Ranger on the guest list. It didn't surprise her that Steve was talking to him as if they were catching up at a high school reunion.

The Ranger stepped away and Steve waited until the only thing heard was the rain pelting against windows overlooking the backyard.

Steve then announced, "We're expecting two more guests, but we'll get started without them. To catch everyone up on what's happened so far, I'll summarize. We believe, but can't prove, that Leonard Spears's former right-hand man, Bill Boyd, conspired with Claire Strobel to kill Dan Clay during the last election. Ms. McBlythe and I weren't engaged to discover if that was true or not, so we didn't pursue that ill-fated event as much as we could have."

Steve turned to Leonard Spears. "Did you tell us that Bill Boyd was in an industrial accident yesterday?"

"That's right."

"To the best of your knowledge, is he still in the hospital?"

"He should be. It was a serious injury to his arm. I also recovered a pistol belonging to Mr. Boyd that the police will be interested in. I believe it's what you call a ghost gun. It appears to be made from a non-metallic substance."

The Ranger spoke up. "Where's the gun now?"

"In the top drawer of my desk, at my warehouse, near the ship channel."

"Will you sign a consent to search?"

"Sure. I'm always happy to help the police."

The Ranger looked at the other law enforcement gathered. "Who wants to conduct the search?"

A man wearing an inexpensive sports coat spoke. "I'll get it and take Mr. Spears with me for questioning. His warehouse is in my patch."

Steve nodded toward the man who'd volunteered. "Thank you, Detective Johnson. I have a few more questions to ask Mr. Spears before you take him."

"Go ahead, Steve. It'll save me some time."

"Mr. Spears," said Steve. "Are you aware of when or where Dan Clay was murdered?"

"I found out by reading the local newspaper when I returned to town."

"Are you saying you were not at the San Jacinto Monument in La Porte on the night of June the seventeenth or eighteenth?"

"I wasn't even in the state."

"Where were you?"

"Vegas. I took a local girl with me for luck. I may have left a lot of cash there but taking her was worth it. She's hard to miss, and I'm sure the casino's cameras were focused on us."

Heather spoke up. "He's telling the truth about the redhead, and the dates he was in Vegas." She tilted her head. "Verify the girl's age. She looks to be about fifteen."

Spears shrugged. "I still say she's good luck. I'm not looking at a murder charge." He added, "Detective Johnson, I may not be too talkative today, but my memory might come back concerning the actions of a certain environmental protester and her involvement in the murder of a political campaign manager. Perhaps my attorney and an assistant DA would enjoy a talk about a plea deal."

Claire shot from her seat and took long strides toward Spears. She got in only one kick to his shin before Leo's partner interceded and made quick work of returning the already hand-cuffed woman to the couch.

Detective Johnson placed his hand on Spear's shoulder. "Let's take a ride. I'll let the officer that came with me cuff you. He has a fifteen-year-old daughter."

The soft murmur of voices filled the room, but only until Steve cleared his throat and said, "Claire, this isn't good for you, and it's going to get worse."

The words had no more left his mouth than Bella and Cindy Clay walked in. Claire shouted, "What are you doing here? You're supposed to be working."

Claire shot an icy stare at Heather. "You're responsible for this. I warned you what would happen if you crossed me."

Heather responded with a smile that was as real as a plastic banana.

Stewart Clay stood. "I'm not sure what's about to happen, but this is my home, and Cindy's my daughter. She's welcome here any time, and you're nothing but a big bag of wind. You've been threatening me and paying protesters to attack my company for years. What has it gotten you? Nothing. I'm worth twice as much now as when you first came after me."

Steve stood and spoke in a calm voice. "Heather, I think it's time we all get comfortable and watched a video. I listened to it three times, and it keeps getting better."

Fred Lawrence no longer had Leonard Spears to watch, so he moved behind Claire and stood with hands clutching the lapels of his open jacket. Meanwhile, Cindy moved to sit beside her father, who allowed her to join him in petting Princess. Their fingers touched, and they exchanged a quick father-daughter glance.

Heather carried on. "My personal assistant recorded what you're about to see and hear. It was yesterday at my office building in The Woodlands. Steve, my PA, and one other witness can attest to its authenticity."

Heather directed everyone's attention to a massive screen. A smattering of chair legs slid on the hardwood floor as everyone sought a better view.

Claire let out a shout of protest and tried to stand. Fred Lawrence grabbed both of her shoulders and unceremoniously pushed her back down onto the couch. "Be nice," he whispered. "The cops can't wait for you to give them a reason to get rough, but they won't need to. I'll do it for them."

The longer the tape played, the more Cindy cried. By the time it was over, Stewart had a firm grip on his daughter's hand and Princess had her head in Cindy's lap.

Heather looked at a woman wearing a business suit with an ID clipped to the lapel. "The last time I checked the federal statutes, extortion was illegal. What do you say, Agents Fuentes and Rainey?"

The female FBI agent said, "The Justice Department still takes a dim view of it. If you're finished with Ms. Strobel, we'll take her off your hands."

The other agent asked, "Are you sure she's not connected to the murder of Dan Clay?"

"Not this murder, but if you dig deep enough, I bet you'll find plenty of other things to charge her with. She may even be willing to tell you some interesting stories about her international connections and her dealings with Leonard Spears."

"Ha," said Claire. "My people will have me out of jail in a few days."

Steve spoke up. "Don't count on it, Claire. You'll be a liability when this video hits the wire services. The oil industry will use you as their best spokesperson for what a true environmental hypocrite looks and sounds like."

"You're blind and crazy."

"No, he's not," said Stewart. "I hired them to investigate, and that's what they did."

Heather spoke up. "Mr. Clay is paying for this investigation. That means he has the right to copies of the evidence we gathered. He can do whatever he wants with it."

"And I want to expose you for the fraud you are."

Heather cast a look toward the two federal agents. "She's all yours if you want to take her now."

The agents looked at each other. "If you don't mind, we're finding this fascinating. Since murder can be a federal and a state crime, it might be best if we stayed to see what else you have."

"Good idea," said Steve.

# Chapter Thirty

Stewart patted his daughter's hand and pushed up from his chair. "Can I get you something to drink?"

"A soft drink, please," said Cindy in her mouse-like voice.

"Do you still drink Dr Pepper?"

"I can't believe you remembered."

Stewart placed a hand on her shoulder. "I insisted we keep some for when you returned."

Heather looked at Bella, who was reaching for a tissue. Prodigals reuniting with their parents always tugged on her heartstrings.

Steve took over. "Anyone else before we resume?"

Lisa stood. "This has been both fascinating and stressful. I'll take a gin and tonic."

All three family members went to the bar and then returned to their seats.

Heather waited until everyone was settled, then said, "Please direct your attention to Mr. Smiley."

Steve remained seated and said, "The murder of Dan Clay is the last item on our agenda today. The case got off to a slow start for law enforcement because the persons responsible carefully planned and executed it. This was an attempt to deceive. It looked like accidental death or suicide, but the deception didn't stop there. A back-up plan was also in place. In fact, three backup plans."

"Three?" asked Stewart.

"That's correct, but we'll put those aside for now. Let's focus on the evidence." He turned his head. "Heather, your turn."

She took a step forward as all eyes focused on her. "Location," she said. "Steve heard on the morning news about a drowning in the middle of the night in the reflection pool at the San Jacinto Monument. He knew the pool wasn't deep enough for an adult to drown in unless it was accidental or intentional. There are three broad types of intentional deaths: suicide, justified, and homicide. Something about the location caused Steve to suspect foul play, so several of our friends joined us and we went to visit the monument. We looked like tourists, but Steve and I, and our dogs, went to look for evidence."

Steve jumped in. "Leo was there, too. We found precious little but left with the feeling that Dan Clay did not kill himself, nor was his death an accident."

"Why not?" asked Lisa

"Mainly intuition," said Steve. "This won't make sense to people who haven't worked as many murders as Heather, Leo and I have, but you get a funny feeling when you go to a crime scene."

Heather quickly added, "We had virtually no details of the event, so Steve called Leo and he met us there with additional information. Dan's car parked on the other side of the road from the reflection pool, in a parking lot. Traffic is very light on that road late at night, so it made sense that park rangers didn't find the body until very early the next morning."

Leo added, "Dan could have parked much closer to the reflection pool, but police found his car in a lot close to the ship channel."

"That seemed odd," said Steve, "because he had to walk a considerable distance through a cemetery and across a road to get to the reflection pool."

"Why was that odd?" asked Stewart.

Heather took her turn. "We didn't know it at the time, but the autopsy showed high levels of drugs and alcohol in his system. Specifically, barbiturates and Scotch whiskey."

Stewart shook his head. "Dan liked his Scotch, but I never knew him to take drugs of any kind."

"The point is," said Steve, "it would have been much easier for Dan to park closer to the pool if he was alone and wanted to harm himself."

Heather added, "The abrasion on his head made it look like he could have dived into the water and struck his head, which supported a preliminary belief of accident or suicide."

Steve then said, "But the coroner now believes someone held him underwater against the rough bottom. The scratches were superficial, no skull fracture or significant hematoma."

It was Heather's turn again. "A search of Dan's car revealed little. In fact, only a mostly empty bottle of Scotch." She paused, "Like I said, the search revealed little. That includes none of Dan's fingerprints on the steering wheel, or the driver's door, both inside and out. However, they did find them on other parts of the car."

Stewart took a shaky breath. "After looking at all the evidence, what did you conclude?"

Heather didn't hesitate. "It was a warm summer night so naturally police found no gloves in the car which could have explained the lack of fingerprints. We concluded that someone else drove Dan's car to the parking lot. He was too impaired to have walked that far to kill himself or commit suicide. A second person took Dan in their car to the pool and drowned him."

Steve waited longer than necessary until he said, "We've confirmed what we suspected. At least two people are responsible for killing Dan Clay."

The members of law enforcement all nodded in agreement as silence fell over the room.

Steve leaned forward and lowered his voice. "The thing that many people forget about evidence is once you know who committed the crime, it's much easier to find more of it."

He leaned back. "Let's turn from the evidence for a while and focus on the deceptions I mentioned earlier. The first and most obvious involved Leonard Spears and his self-confessed grudge against Dan. After all, they were political foes and Spears's enforcer killed Dan's campaign manager."

Stewart bristled. "He might not have killed Dan, but I still say he ordered Bill Boyd to kill Dan's campaign manager."

"Heather and I won't argue that point. However, you turned your home into an armed fortress and came very close to declaring war on Spears. Did you ever consider that's exactly what the people who killed Dan wanted you to do? If things escalated, someone was bound to get hurt or killed. It was only a matter of time."

Steve added, "The police would have come down on you and Spears. The investigation of Dan's murder would have moved to the back of the file cabinet."

Leo spoke up. "Steve's right, Mr. Clay. The case might have someday gotten some attention, but not until everyone involved stopped playing like characters in a remake of *The Godfather*. Whatever gets the biggest and most recent headlines gets the most immediate attention."

"Thanks, Leo," said Steve. "The point is, Mr. Clay, your words and actions almost played into the killers' hands." He allowed the words to settle and added, "But you didn't go after Spears, and we now know that you'd have been wrong if you or your men had attacked him."

Lisa spoke up from across the room. "Didn't you say Claire Strobel was in league with Mr. Spears?"

"I'm glad you brought that up," said Steve. "We believe she was—"

Claire cut him off. "You'll never prove it."

"Don't bet on it," said Leo. "I had a little chat with Bill Boyd in the hospital last night. He wasn't very pleased that Mr. Spears has no further use for his services and he's now looking at going back to prison on a gun charge. He was most cooperative when I asked him about the location of various illegal substances. It seems Mr. Spears has quite a few small storage spaces we didn't know about."

"So? He's a petty criminal. That doesn't concern me."

"Not according to Bill Boyd. He says your involvement with Leonard Spears goes back a long time and is still going on. Spears will want to make a deal by this time tomorrow." Leo chuckled. "When you sleep with dogs, you get fleas."

Steve gave Le Roi a pat on the head. "Present company excluded." He sat up straight. "Let's get back to Dan's murder. Claire Strobel was the second distraction. She was the back-up suspect after Leonard Spears. She hates big oil and Dan was the heir apparent to take over Clay Oil. Even though she's a fraud and a hypocrite with a long history of inciting violence, she didn't kill Dan. She might have known about the plot, but Heather and I don't think so."

"Why not?" asked Stewart.

"The plot to kill your son goes much deeper, and yet, the motives behind it are old and often repeated."

Heather jumped in. "Love and money."

Steve shrugged. "Money for sure. Sometimes it's hard to tell the difference between love and lust."

He allowed the words to percolate before saying. "Let's get back to the evidence found in Dan's car. Who remembers what it was?"

The female FBI agent said, "No gloves, no fingerprints on the driver's side, and a bottle of Scotch."

"Excellent," said Steve. "It was an almost empty bottle of Johnny Walker Black Label Scotch whiskey."

"Black label," shouted Stewart. "Dan and I drink blue label." He paused. "At least we used to drink it together."

Lisa asked, "What's the difference?"

Steve shrugged. "Nothing to most people, but to those with a discerning palate, it makes a tremendous difference. I'm told it's because of the rarity of the cask it's aged in."

"That's right," said Stewart. "Dan wouldn't drink anything but blue label, Texas edition. It's about $250.00 a bottle, while the same bottle of black label is about $50.00."

Steve lifted his chin. "Heather and I asked each other who knew Dan well enough to know he liked to drink Johnny Walker Blue Label?"

"I knew," said Stewart.

"Me, too," said Cindy.

"Very good," said Steve.

"I knew," said Lisa.

"Anyone else?" asked Steve.

No one responded, so Steve asked, "What about you, Fred? As head of security, you should have known."

"Me? I stay busy looking for threats, not memorizing the labels on whiskey bottles."

"That's interesting. I'd have thought a former CIA operative would have noticed something like that. Perhaps that's the reason they let you go."

By this time, Heather had inched back to where she was beyond Fred's peripheral vision.

Steve kept talking to the bodyguard. "Do you remember what Heather said was the motive for Dan's murder? It was love AND money, but I said it's sometimes hard to distinguish love from lust." He leaned down and whispered something to Le Roi, causing him to bare his teeth and let out a low growl. Princess heard the command and bared her teeth, too.

Heather pulled her pistol from the holster on her hip. "I have my pistol trained on you, Fred. There are two dogs who would like nothing more than to chew you to bits. Be a good boy and don't make any sudden moves."

"What? You think I had something to do with killing Mr. Clay's son?"

Half a dozen pistols came from under jackets and an ornately engraved .45 came out of the Texas Ranger's holster. He advanced to within six feet of Fred. "Hands on your head."

"You're going to believe this washed-up, has-been detective?" Fred asked incredulously.

Leo holstered his weapon and took out a pair of handcuffs. "Yes, we are believing him." With handcuffs secured, Leo removed Fred's pistol from its shoulder holster.

Heather said, "There's at least one more on him, and I bet there's two."

Leo found both. The Ranger circled the couch and took off Fred's belt. He found a four-inch, slender knife in it.

Heather said, "There's a metal-detecting wand on the table in the entryway. You'd better give him a good once-over before you leave."

Steve asked, "Can I continue?"

"Go ahead," said Heather. "We're three out of four so far."

"Love and money," said Steve. "As you can see, we're down to two family members and the man who hired us to discover who killed his son. They are the only ones who knew Dan well enough for him to trust them. We ruled out Stewart right away. It made no sense for him to allow us to investigate Dan's murder if he was involved in killing his son. After all, Dan was going to inherit the oil company."

"Remember," said Heather. "We already established that it took two people to murder Dan. One to ply him with alcohol and drugs, load him into a car, take him to the monument, and drown him. That one was Fred Lawrence."

"Right," said Steve, "and one more person to take his car to the monument and leave it in the parking lot overlooking the ship channel."

"Love and money," said Heather.

Leo broke in. "All right, you two. We're all listening. Was it Dan's stepmother or his sister who helped kill him?"

Heather watched as Stewart took his daughter's hand and held on tightly as Steve announced. "Princess gave us the first clue."

Fred once again found his voice. "If you think I'm taking the blame for something I wasn't involved in, you're all nuts. Cindy and her stepmother planned to kill Dan and split the inheritance after Stewart kicked the bucket, which will happen much sooner than any of you think."

Leo rolled his eyes. "Steve, I know Heather went to Galveston to interview Cindy. Are you saying she found out that Cindy and Lisa killed Dan?"

Cindy let out a gasp.

Steve's head moved back and forth. "Of course not. Cindy was the killer's third diversion, their last line of defense. The only thing Cindy is guilty of is not being able to stand up for herself. Princess had no trouble identifying her as a victim who needs love."

Steve pointed at Lisa. "We first suspected you and Fred

had something going on when you left this compound to go to Lake Conroe to look at our lake homes. You two jumped at the chance to look for properties for yourselves. After narrowing it down to two homes, you wanted a large home on a golf course."

Stewart broke in. "I overrode her selection and went for the smaller home on the lake. I'm glad I didn't give in to her."

Lisa raised her chin, her look defiant. "There's one thing you're neglecting, Mr. Smiley. Evidence."

Stewart spoke up. "I'll give this Texas Ranger all he needs. Fred put cameras everywhere. He was so arrogant and sure I trusted him, that he became careless, but I made copies he doesn't know about. When Steve said it's sometimes hard to tell the difference between love and lust, I have plenty of proof of the latter. There will be no doubt in their minds what was going on between the two of you."

Steve added. "Remember what I said about once you know who committed the crime, it's easier to find evidence. These officers will find out if it was Lisa or Fred who bought the Johnny Walker Black Label."

"It was Fred," shouted Lisa.

"Shut up," said Fred through gritted teeth.

"No, I won't. It was all your idea."

Heather's gaze traveled around the collection of law enforcement officers gathered in the room. "Gentlemen, I believe you have another customer."

Leo motioned for an officer to take Lisa into custody. The co-conspirators were led from the room, their shouts of protest and blame echoing through the foyer. A third officer escorted Claire Strobel from the room.

Stewart looked at Heather. "Would you mind getting the keys to the lake house back from Lisa? She no longer has need of a love nest."

Heather reached into the pocket of her jacket. "The keys

241

you gave Lisa won't open anything. Here are the keys to your home."

Steve said, "We're looking forward to having you as a neighbor."

Bella took Cindy's hand. "That goes for me and Adam, too."

Heather delivered the keys and looked at Cindy and then her father. "All you two need is a couple of special dogs. We know the perfect place to get them."

"Oh, Daddy. Can I?"

"Only if you'll let me visit you at your lake house."

"Visit? Why can't we live there together?"

For the first time that day, Stewart smiled. "We'll go tomorrow and buy all new furniture."

# Chapter Thirty-One

Heather asked Steve if he needed help to get into the passenger side of her new golf cart.

"No, thanks. Le Roi and I practiced while you were changing clothes. He understands dogs ride in the back seat. Muddy paws and light-colored shorts are a terrible combination. You were wise to get washable slipcovers for the seats."

Heather gave a command to Princess, and the dog joined Le Roi in what looked like their first royal parade in a golf cart.

"Someday soon," said Steve, "I'll get my own."

"What a fabulous idea," said Heather. "You could go to the recreation center to attend classes, go to the library, join the senior swim team, or just ride around the development."

"I could also go to the convenience store and get a pint of ice cream whenever I wanted."

"Only after you burn the calories you're going to gain."

What she didn't tell him was she'd already ordered an autonomous cart for him. Semi-freedom was not far away, thanks to technology.

Steve asked, "How far away did you say Stewart and Cindy's home is?"

"About twelve minutes by golf cart. It's at the far end of the development. In fact, it's the last lakefront home before the national forest."

"It sounds peaceful."

"Too quiet for most people," said Heather. "But Cindy couldn't be happier. Bella checks in with her every day."

"What about Stewart? I feel bad for not calling him."

"I've only talked to him once since we finished the case. He's been wrapping up things in Houston, so we should get a report on how things are progressing this afternoon."

The short drive passed in silence as Heather alternated between admiring the scenery and looking in the rearview mirror. The wind had Le Roi's ears swept back and his beard fluttering. Princess sat up straight and proud. All that was missing was for her dog to raise a paw and wave at the adoring squirrels they passed.

Bella and Adam's golf cart sat in the driveway, and Heather parked beside it. All four occupants of her new ride unloaded and made their way to the front door. It swung open before Heather's finger touched the doorbell.

After a step back and a double take at the smiling young woman who answered the door, Heather closed her gaping mouth. "Cindy? Is that you?"

Bella appeared over Cindy's shoulder. "Doesn't she look totally amazing? We had a spa day yesterday, complete with a full makeover."

Cindy spun in a circle and fluffed out her hair. "I'm still getting used to the look, but I love it. The hair is short enough to wash and dry after a long walk in the woods, but long enough that I don't look like a boy."

Heather looked at the firm legs protruding from summer

shorts and the curves that weren't hidden under a baggy dress. "Keep dressing like that and no one will accuse you of being anything but a beautiful woman."

"I didn't know what freedom felt like until I got out from under Claire's thumb and told the police everything she did to me. The haircut and clothes symbolize the new me."

Bella said, "You should have seen the guys staring at her when we went to the pool at the recreation center this morning."

A pleasant rose color filled Cindy's cheeks as she said, "Please, come in. I'm being a terrible hostess."

Stewart's voice sounded from somewhere beyond the modest entryway. "Is that you, Steve?"

"*C'est moi,* as Le Roi would say if he could talk."

"There's a dog headed your way."

Heather watched as a butterscotch and white cocker spaniel ran toward them and slid to a stop in front of Princess. Cindy scooped him up in her arms. "Isn't Graham the most handsome thing you've ever seen?"

Steve said, "Graham? I like it. It's a unique name for a dog."

"Daddy helped me name him. It seems I ate a lot of graham crackers when I was growing up. His coloring reminded him of my favorite snack and milk."

Heather couldn't keep herself from running a hand over the floppy ears. "He's stunning, and a spaniel is the perfect dog for you. Are you getting another to keep him company?"

"Not yet. Dad's still looking for what he wants."

The group migrated to the living room where all but Steve took in its killer view of the lake. Stewart jumped into the conversation as he joined them. "I always wanted a black lab, but I'm not in a hurry to get one."

Heather thought this was an interesting statement, considering his deteriorating physical condition. He must have seen the question in her gaze.

"Let's everyone have a seat. I have what amounts to a confession to make. I've already told Cindy, but I misled Heather on the day she and Steve solved Dan's murder."

The ringing of the doorbell put the conversation on hold. Cindy and Graham ran to the door. A muffled conversation followed. Rasheed entered the room. "My most sincere apologies for being tardy. It is said that being late is expected of a sloth, but not a man."

"Come in, Rasheed," said Stewart. "I've heard you're a man of exceptional wisdom. I'd like to get to know you better. Do you live in the development?"

"As of today, I do. In a condo close to the entrance. Setting up my bed took longer than I anticipated."

"Outstanding. Do you play chess?"

"I find it stimulating even though I lose with alarming frequency."

"That's perfect. We'll be well matched."

The doorbell rang again, and Cindy and her furry shadow once again hurried to the front door. The conversation didn't last long.

Heather came out of her seat when she saw who the visitor was. "Junani? What's wrong?"

Heather moved toward her while saying. "This is Junani Hasan, the most recent addition to my legal staff."

Puffy eyes met Heather's questioning gaze. Junani held up a hand like a stop sign. "Forgive the intrusion, but please, Ms. McBlythe I have something to say to Rasheed that can wait no longer. It is to my great shame I must say it before my courage takes flight."

Stewart spoke with a Texas drawl. "Go ahead, young lady. Whatever it is, get it off your chest."

Junani took a step toward Rasheed and stopped. "You must listen to me, Rasheed. You hurt me deeply the night of our date at the French restaurant."

"I... uh..."

She cut him off. "It was not the spilled ratatouille, or the ruined dress, or even your clumsy attempt to wipe the stain from my lap."

"I don't understand."

She choked on the next words and had to clear her throat. "You abandoned me. That stabbed my heart and now I bleed tears. I will tolerate much from you but leaving me is something you must never do again. Do you understand?"

"Uh... uh..."

Steve shouted, "The answer is *yes*. Say it!"

"Yes, yes, YES!"

Rasheed seemed to go to her without his feet touching the ground. For once, he said nothing while guiding her out of the room. The front door slammed shut.

The room remained as silent as an empty church until Stewart said, "That beats anything I ever saw. That woman has more brass than a three-hundred-member marching band. I like her spunk."

Cindy took her turn. "I do, too."

Stewart kept talking. "With any luck, I'll finish what I need to say without another interruption. Like I said before, I misled Heather when we were closing the deal on this house. I suspected Lisa and Fred of killing Dan all along, but I had to make sure. I purposely let it slip to Lisa that I had cancer and only a short time to live. This caused my future ex-wife and bodyguard to get careless. Steve and Heather both knew something was going on when the two love birds came to this development and picked out a home. Lisa was planning to be a grieving widow for a while and then marry Fred. With Dan out of the way and Cindy being hoodwinked by Claire Strobel, Lisa was sure I'd leave most everything to her."

Steve spoke up. "But Princess diagnosed you with cancer. I bet that was a shock."

"More than a shock. It scared me so much I couldn't think straight. Luckily, you and Heather did the thinking for me and turned Lisa and Fred against each other. You also took care of Leonard Spears, Bill Boyd, and Claire Strobel along the way."

Heather asked, "What about the cancer?"

Cindy spoke with excitement driving her words. "It's completely treatable. The doctors expect a full recovery, thanks to early detection."

"One more thing," said Heather. "Are you still selling your oil company?"

Stewart ran the palm of his hand across his chin. "I wasn't sure when I told you that, but now I am. The oil business is rough in every way. As things stand now, I'm freer of enemies than I've been since I drilled my first well. I like the way it feels. I'm getting out and will enjoy the rest of my life with my daughter."

Cindy's eyes sparkled. "We're getting solar panels and Dad's getting an electric bicycle like mine."

Stewart added, "Cindy wants a hybrid car and I'm in the market for a hybrid truck."

"That's a great compromise," said Steve. "If Rasheed was here, he'd have a parable for us."

Stewart chuckled. "Something tells me being around that long-legged gal will spur him on to write plenty of parables about making compromises."

## FROM THE AUTHOR

Thank you for reading *Murder At The Monument*. I hope you enjoyed your escape to an iconic Texas monument as you turned the pages to find out whodunit! If you loved it, please consider leaving a review at your favorite retailer, Bookbub or Goodreads. YOUR review could be the one that helps another mystery lover discover their next great book!

To stay abreast of Smiley and McBlythe's latest adventure, and all my book news, join my Mystery Insiders community. As a thank you, I'll send you a *reader exclusive* Smiley and McBlythe mystery novella!

You can also follow me on Amazon, Bookbub and Goodreads to receive notification of my latest release.

Happy reading!
Bruce

Scan the image to sign up or go to brucehammack.com/the-smiley-and-mcblythe-mysteries-reader-gift/

# ABOUT THE AUTHOR

Bruce Hammack, a native Texan, began his professional writing career in the tenth grade when the local Lions Club sponsored a writing contest for students in civics class. To the amazement of students and teachers alike, he won the prize of a twenty-five-dollar savings bond.

After retiring from a career in criminal justice, Bruce picked up the proverbial pen again. He now draws on his extensive background with law enforcement (and criminals) to write contemporary, clean read detective and crime mysteries.

Bruce has lived in a total of eighteen cities around the country and the world, but now calls the Texas hill country home with his wife of thirty-plus years. When not writing, he enjoys reading a classic mystery, watching whodunits, and travel.

---

Follow Bruce on Amazon, Facebook, Instagram, Bookbub or Goodreads for the latest new release info and recommendations. Learn more at brucehammack.com.

Made in the USA
Coppell, TX
10 July 2025

51741789R00152